DISCARD

D1562670

AFTER OZ

ALSO AVAILABLE BY GORDON MCALPINE

Holmes Entangled
Woman with a Blue Pencil
Mystery Box
The Persistence of Memory
Joy in Mudville

The Misadventures of Edgar and Allan Poe series
The Pet and the Pendulum
Once Upon a Midnight Eerie
The Tell-Tale Start

AFTER OZ

A NOVEL

Gordon McAlpine

CROOKED
LANE

NEW YORK

Published in the United States by Crooked Lane Books, an imprint of The Quick Brown Fox & Company LLC.

Crooked Lane Books and its logo are trademarks of The Quick Brown Fox & Company LLC.

Library of Congress Catalog-in-Publication data available upon request.

ISBN (hardcover): 978-1-63910-785-8
ISBN (ebook): 978-1-63910-786-5

Cover design by Heather VenHuizen

Printed in the United States.

www.crookedlanebooks.com

Crooked Lane Books
34 West 27th St., 10th Floor
New York, NY 10001

First Edition: August 2024

10 9 8 7 6 5 4 3 2 1

For Kieran, whenever you're ready . . .

Part One

"Thou liftest me up to the wind; thou causest me to ride upon it, and dissolvest my substance."

—Job 30:22

CHAPTER 1

Regarding the events of late June and July 1896

Sunbonnet, Kansas

Immediately after the twister, we townsfolk occupied ourselves with the demands of our particular situations, rounding up livestock we'd set loose from our barns and corrals at first sight of the approaching funnel, repairing roofs where shingles had been ripped away, righting and attempting to salvage the overturned farm equipment that littered our fields like great dead locusts. Some of us had been left with little more than rubble to comb through—houses, windmills, corncribs, barns, and granaries pulverized; personal items, such as clothing, photographs, and pages from family Bibles indiscriminately scattered into cornfields from here to the county line. And there was injury and loss of life too. The blacksmith's wife suffered lacerations to her face and arms when a window exploded into shards. The postmaster's son broke his leg when a rotted stair in the storm cellar gave way and cast him onto the hard dirt floor. Jeb Harling's prize heifer was found in a cornfield, her head severed from her shoulder as cleanly as if by a guillotine. But even with all this, we were most concerned with the disappearance of the eleven-year-old Gale girl.

Orphaned shortly after birth, raised by her aunt and uncle, dreamy, distant, difficult, not altogether well liked by her classmates, young Dorothy had last been seen by her Aunt Emily the moment before the twister hit the house. By then Emily had taken refuge across the yard in the storm cellar. She had thought Dorothy was elsewhere. Contrary to what townswomen said in the days after the twister, Emily had not been neglectful of her niece. Before racing from the house to the storm cellar, Emily had run from room to room, calling, "Dorothy? Dorothy!" Characteristically, the girl had chosen the worst possible moment to disappear. She was likely out picking flowers in the rain or some such nonsense. So what else could the poor woman do but seek safety ahead of the twister? Wasn't that second nature to anyone raised on the prairie? Except Dorothy, apparently.

Still, the girl remained foremost on her aunt's mind.

That's why, even as the twister drew nearer, its path still drunken, Emily remained exposed atop the storm cellar stairs, struggling against the wind to hold the two hinged doors open above her like some strange wooden-winged creature. She wasn't going to slip into the relative calm of the cellar with the girl still unaccounted for. Dust and debris whipped her face. Emily had never felt more afraid. Or alone—her niece gone; her husband in town at the general store; and the family's three farmhands, Zeb, Scrub, and Rusty, off the property. They'd left mid-afternoon, all three dressed like fools in store-bought shirts, hard shoes, and Stetsons for what they thought would be an ordinary Saturday evening of drinking spirits and getting up to no good. No one had expected a sudden accumulation of storm clouds. Tornado season was supposed to have passed.

It hadn't.

Then, through the swirling chaos, Emily thought she saw Dorothy *inside the farmhouse*, darting recklessly from window to window. Where had the girl come from? Where had she been? Why hadn't she answered when her aunt had called for her in the house? And why didn't she get herself across the farmyard to the storm cellar? Or was the movement Emily glimpsed in the house just the swirling of curtains? She couldn't be sure. She shouted Dorothy's name, though she thought it unlikely the girl could have heard her in the din. So the woman screwed her courage to the sticking point and started up the cellar steps, determined to fight her way across the wind-beaten farmyard to look once more for the foolhardy girl. But a sudden gust slammed the wooden doors shut atop her, casting her down the short stairwell. Fortunate not to have been hurt, she pulled herself up in the darkness and climbed the stairs once more, but now when she pushed on the doors she could no longer open them against the wind. Finally, Emily could do nothing but huddle alone on the earthen floor as the twister grew loud as a locomotive just outside. She wept and prayed. Then the thing grew louder yet. No mere train anymore. "Armageddon," she said to us in the days after the twister and before the seizure that would strip her of speech. "That's what it sounded like." Fire and brimstone and wild, raging beasts for which there are no known names.

And the sound was not the worst of it.

★ ★ ★

By the time the first group of us arrived—less than two hours after Emily had climbed out of the storm cellar, less than an hour after her husband Henry had returned to the property directly from town—it was apparent that the twister had pulled the family's house from its foundation, spun it a quarter turn, then slammed it back to earth, dashing it to bits. We'd seen structures destroyed by twisters before. This is, after all, tornado alley. But the Gale house looked different, almost as if it had been dropped from a great height, the debris gathered in a single giant pile rather than scattered across the fields. We joined Henry and Emily in their search through the wreckage, pulling and lifting away shattered wood, broken glass, and twisted metal. We worked with urgency. But we found no sign of the girl's remains. Not a hair from her head, a scrap of her gingham dress, nor a drop of blood.

There's no sense denying that we all grew up on tales of folks pulled bodily into the funnel of a twister—higher, higher, higher—only to be delivered back to earth many miles away, dropped onto a haystack without even a scratch, miraculously alive. Having long since left such childish yarns behind, we knew that the reality of being pulled up into the funnel of a tornado was akin to standing in an open field between the massed artillery of Meade and Lee at Gettysburg and enduring multiple well-aimed blasts of their cannons.

Yet, as I say, no pieces of the girl's body were found among the rubble.

Occupied as we were with our own damage and tribulations, we still maintained hope that eleven-year-old Dorothy might have run out of the farmhouse in the seconds between the storm cellar doors slamming shut on her aunt and the arrival of the pulverizing funnel. Gathering later that evening, in twos and threes, in the lesser wreckage of our own properties, we debated the girl's prospects. There'd have been nothing for her to note in any direction on the flat horizon except the black wall of clouds in the south and the twister upright and dancing like a charmed snake. So it was not implausible that she might have run across her family's sorghum patch in the direction of the corn crib, which was untouched by the twister, and continued on toward the small grove of box-elder trees that grew wild near the watering hole a half mile away. Of course, a grove is no shelter from a tornado, but only another source of potential shrapnel, sheared wood being as efficient at tearing through a body as metal. But the mind doesn't work that way when the wrath of the Lord is at hand. Besides, when all else is just empty horizon (or, worse, banks of murderous clouds), what call would the girl have to run in any *other* direction? So the next day, immediately after Sunday service, a dozen of us organized to search the fields for any sign of the child. We aligned ourselves thirty yards apart and proceeded from the demolished farmhouse, through the sorghum, all the way past the watering hole, and on to the road. We discovered nothing. Not a footprint, not a hair ribbon, not a shoe—not even any sign of the girl's little dog, which had disappeared along with her.

★   ★   ★

"It's a mystery," Henry said to us when we returned to his farmyard, empty-handed, from our search for his niece. He'd not joined us in the search, but had continued picking through the wreckage of his house. There wasn't much left to be salvaged. Now, with news of our failure, he looked up at the sky, which was gray but no longer threatening. After a moment, the willowy man offered us well water, saying nothing more about his missing niece. His gaze broke from ours every few seconds, turning again and again to the pile of junk that had been his home. His expression seemed more one of wonder than despair. But we knew better than to believe it.

His wife, Emily, had taken ill and was now lying abed at a neighbor's place. She blamed herself for having left her niece in the house, and so she refused to eat or drink.

"Damn fool woman," Henry said when we asked after her.

Henry had been away when the twister hit, so he considered himself blameless for his niece's disappearance. Or almost blameless.

"Guess I could've placed the storm cellar nearer the house," he muttered as we put our hands in our pockets and shuffled our feet in the dusty yard, gestures intended to ease our imminent leave-taking. "Or better yet, I could've built the house where the corn crib is, could've done that easily enough when I built it in the first place, all those years ago. Why not? One spot's same as the other. Then I wouldn't have no problems now. I should've put it there. Didn't. But should have."

"Nonsense." Reverend Richter stepped forward to reassure him. The reverend was the logical choice when it came to offering reassurances. His sermon that morning had been full of them.

"Nonsense?" Henry turned to the reverend, who was a full head taller, luxuriantly bearded, and possessed of learning and gravity that Henry either failed to note or disregarded. He allowed no time for an answer. "Yeah, 'nonsense' is the right word." He glanced away but continued speaking. "Right word for *all* of it, Reverend. Nonsense . . ."

"Let's not lose heart, Henry," the reverend said. "You know despair is a sin."

Henry blew a long, weary breath through his puckered lips, making a slight whistling sound. "Who said anything about despair? I believe your word was 'nonsense,' Reverend."

"I meant it in regard to your—"

Henry didn't let him finish. "*I* meant it, Reverend, in regard to every splintered piece of wood here in this yard, every blasted fragment of rubble that lifted itself up yesterday and then dropped back to earth like it had never been part of no hungry beast. But it *had* been. All this you see around you, down to the soil we're standing on, was the very teeth of the monster. Sure, now it's just dirt and dust and broke pieces of trees and the things I built with my own hands. And, yeah, now we got to go forward and remake our lives. Even though we know now what the earth and the air itself will do to us if given the chance . . . rise up and *scythe us down.*" He kicked at a pebble barely bigger than a buckshot and sent it skipping across the hard dirt. "Peaceable kingdom? Bah! It's nonsense. The whole world is nonsense."

We'd never heard Henry say such things. Actually, we'd never heard anyone speak so disrespectfully to the reverend.

To make matters worse, it was a Sunday, not three hours gone since the reverend had cited Isaiah from the pulpit, reminding us that God promises a *"refuge and shelter from the storm and rain."* Henry hadn't been at the service. No one blamed him or Emily for missing it, considering their circumstances. This was no ordinary Sunday. Many others were absent that morning. But some had made the effort despite their tribulations. Naturally, we didn't expect or require it of anyone. But now we worried about Henry. Seemed he could have used the word of the Lord more than most.

Reverend Richter silently considered this profane outburst, then placed his hand on Henry's shoulder. "Henry, this world, broken as it may seem, is not 'nonsense.'" The reverend spoke with a slight accent he'd acquired in his years away from here at the seminary. The cadence had elements of the South, of the passionate delivery of the Baptist preacher. Meantime, his pronunciation hinted of New England, where the seeds of Protestantism had sprung up three centuries before. In all, a remarkable combination considering that the seminary was in Indianapolis. "Only the ways of Man can be nonsense. For example, your self-recriminations about the placement of your house. That's all I was saying. Or the despairing way you chose to see our blessed earth just now. If you don't mind my saying so, your dismissal of this Divine gift of inestimable value . . . well, *that's* nonsense, Henry."

Henry looked at his shoes, but he remained agitated.

"Consider Jeremiah 29:11." The reverend spoke as if he were back in the pulpit. "*'I know the plans I have for you, declares the Lord, plans for welfare and not for evil, to give you a future and a hope.'* You understand, Henry? Future and hope. The way of the Lord is never nonsense. The way of the Lord is Providence. Even when we don't understand His workings."

"If I remember my geography rightly, Providence is a town in Rhode Island," Henry answered.

We were all of us further taken aback.

In days to come, this moment of weakness would darkly color the town's view of Henry.

"There's no call to be blasphemous," said Carson Whitfield, stepping out from among us. Whitfield was a cattle buyer and represented a line of grain elevators along the railroad to the east, so he often traveled to glamorous cities like St. Louis or Chicago. Few of us, besides the reverend, had ever ventured so far. He was short, round, and bald, but his commercial enterprise made him one of the most admired men in the county. "We understand your anguish. None of us blame you for being rash. Your niece's disappearance is worrisome indeed. But that's still no call for you to—"

"My niece?" Henry shook his head, as if confused.

Sheriff Hutchins, a thickly built man of fifty who dressed more nattily than any lawman this side of Bat Masterson, spoke next. "We're going to find her, Henry. Don't let your worry drive you to say godless things you don't believe. We'll find her."

"You're sure to find her, Sheriff. A girl don't just disappear into thin air. She'll turn up. Do you think that's what's troubling me?" He turned and indicated with an exaggerated wave of his arm the demolished farmhouse. "Are you all blind? I'm nearly sixty-three years old. My house is matchsticks. My fields are half ruined. My livestock is wandering the county. I'm a farmer. Look at what I've left to farm."

"Property can be repaired," the sheriff said. "Livestock can be replaced. The girl is the pressing matter."

"The girl will turn up," Henry snapped. Then he turned to his farmhands. Zeb, Scrub, and Rusty had joined in our fruitless search through the fields. At first word of the twister the evening before, they'd raced back to the farmstead, each still dressed in his going-to-town clothes, to help dig through the wreckage. They worked alongside Henry through the night, sorting and piling by the light of kerosene lamps. We arrived late morning to organize the search. It was only then the three went to the barn to change into work clothes. Now, when Henry waggled his hand at them, they stepped forward as if drawn by a string. "You boys get after the livestock." He swept his arm toward the barn, the corral, and the pigpens, all untouched by the twister. Emily might as well never have let loose the now-wandering animals. "It's like the Lord was laughing at us last night. Get to it, boys. Round 'em up. There'll be no more lollygagging." He turned away from us, starting for his wrecked house, as if something remained inside it to reclaim. As if there *were* an inside. "Thank you all for your help," he called without turning around. "But don't worry. The girl's obstinate. She'll turn up."

We made our way back to our own families.

★   ★   ★

That neither hide nor hair of the girl was discovered within a two-mile radius of the Gale farm was no reflection on our determination; rather, it seemed a mystery so inscrutable it was otherworldly. Regardless of outcome, the searching provided us with the immediate relief of taking action. When an eleven-year-old girl disappears into thin air, the need to do *something* takes over. But do what? It was the daily gatherings of volunteers that gave us purpose, whether or not Henry Gale joined us even once in the search.

"She's bound to turn up," Sheriff Hutchins would say, echoing Henry's last words to us, but with hope rather than dismissiveness. The sheriff had always been a competent and decent man, qualities highly regarded in Sunbonnet.

But as the first day of searching turned to a second and then a third, and Dorothy Gale remained unaccounted for, the possibility of her turning up alive became less likely. Just as we knew that tales of twisters gently delivering folks from one place to another was mere schoolyard lore, we also knew that sometimes bodies *were* lifted into the funnel of a twister to be ravaged and then dropped, usually in many pieces, miles away. We never disagreed with Henry or the sheriff that we'd find the girl. Most likely, however, we'd find her in the branches of one or more trees or floating face down in a mud hole or smashed headfirst up to her waist into hard clay. Such occurrences were not prairie tall tales, but counted among the personal reminiscences of most of us, death by tornado being not uncommon in our parts. With so much livestock still wandering the prairie and hungry coyotes stalking the land, none of us *wanted* to be the one to find whatever remained of the girl. But as we were decent folk, we weren't put off. The girl had to be found. And better by one of us than by wild animals or our own children.

We remained resolved.

As it turned out, we did come across a body. It didn't belong to the Gale girl. But that's getting ahead of events as they occurred.

CHAPTER 2

Topeka Insane Asylum, Topeka, Kansas—September 1896

The grounds are parklike, suggestive of healthful living, though few of the patients partake of the outdoors. Those few who do are accompanied by burly attendants who carry riding crops as tools of discipline, or are roped together in groups of four or more, being of torpid disposition. A long drive leads from the road to the five-story main building. Viewed from the front, the asylum resembles a grand Victorian mansion, complete with a wide porch, balconies, many windows, and attractively decorated turrets. In accordance with the Kirkbride Plan, four separate wings radiate out from the main building. These enormous wings bear an institutional appearance, being made of granite, as favored by the Chicago School of architecture. Inside, the facility is clean and exhibits few of the signs of obvious neglect that characterized Blackwell's Island or other notorious madhouses. Since Nelly Bly publicized such circumstances, institutions have grown more subtle in their abuses. Unfortunately, the general living conditions, while sanitary, still adhere to an archaic treatment plan that requires patients to spend many hours a day sitting in rocking chairs that line the hallways, one placed directly in front of the next. No talking is permitted. For all the beauty of the grounds, most patients do not even enjoy a view out of a window during these endless hours. Any sane man or woman would grow mad in a matter of months, considering such soul-deadening practices of intellectual and physical denial.

Or any child.

There is no children's wing. Dorothy G. is kept alone in a room near the institutionalized women who are pregnant or nursing newborns. The girl is thought of as dangerous and has no contact with the young women or babies. In her room is a bed, a chamber pot, a small bureau for her handful of possessions, a doll's house (but no dolls), and a few books donated by a church charity. These books include the Bible, which contains many scenes that could be considered morally objectionable for an eleven-year-old girl, particularly one given to fancy. Although, in the interest of occupying her clearly active mind, I would not dream of removing any book from her.

A nurse in a black dress, white cap, and large apron jangled a handful of keys as she led me down a long corridor to the dining hall, the interior walls scrubbed to a whiteness found only in public institutions. Her charge was to take me to Dorothy G. "Positively demented, the girl," the nurse said. "A hopeless case." I reminded her that her job included neither diagnosis nor prognosis. She huffed and spoke not another word. No doubt she viewed me as an overeducated and arrogant bluestocking, a traitor to our sex. Nothing new there. The nurse left me alone in the deserted dining hall with Dorothy, then locked us in.

Dorothy G. is a slight girl who looks younger than her eleven years. Perhaps she has lost weight since her arrival here.

Given the poor quality of the meals—dinner consists of a tin plate of cold boiled meat and a small, undercooked potato—I wouldn't be surprised. When I met her, she wore an underskirt made of coarse dark cotton and a cheap white calico dress that had a large gray stain. Her hair was tied in one plait with a red cotton rag. When she spoke, she exhibited an intelligence that belies her tender age. Fortunately, it seems her mind has not yet succumbed to this place. However, her persistent conviction that the hallucination that brought her here, and inspired my trip as well, is real and has not abated.

The following is reconstructed from notes taken at the time:

"Dorothy is a very nice name."

"Thank you."

"I stopped at the Topeka Public Library before coming here, and do you know what I discovered?"

"You can discover lots of things in a library. How would I know?"

"I discovered that the name *Dorothy* means 'gift of God.' It comes from the ancient Greek. Isn't that lovely?

". . ."

"What's wrong?"

"Nobody back home thinks I'm a gift from God. If they ever did."

"What people think, or don't think, isn't necessarily right or true."

"Now you sound like my aunt."

"Does that bother you?"

"Where is my aunt? Why hasn't she ever come here? It's been quite a long time."

"Do you know how long you've been in this place?"

"No."

"How long does it seem to you? Days? Weeks? Months?"

"Years."

"That long?"

"No, not really. It seems like weeks. Maybe four? I haven't been keeping track. How long has it been?"

"Close to two months."

"Am I getting out now?"

"Not yet."

"Am I ever getting out?"

"I'm here to help see that you do. But you have to be patient."

"I'm not supposed to be patient, I'm eleven years old."

"You have a point there, Dorothy."

"Even if I *am* a patient."

"Very good. Clever."

"Who are you?"

"I'm Evelyn Grace Wilford. I'm a doctor."

"I didn't know a lady could be a doctor. Especially one who's not old and withered. You must not be from around here."

"I'm from New York. But I've lived in Boston the past few years."

"I've heard of those places. I've never been to a city, except for . . ."

"Except for?"

"Never mind."

"The Emerald City?"

"So you know about that. I guess you would since you're a doctor and you're here, talking to me."

"Will you tell me about the Emerald City?"

"I'd rather not. Tell me about New York and Boston."

"What about them?"

"How are they different?"

"That's an interesting question. I guess I'd say New York is noisier. And Boston is colder."

"They don't sound very nice."

"Well, neither is exactly *nice*. But they're both filled with interesting things. Interesting people."

"I prefer cold to noise. Is that why you went to Boston?"

"I went there to study medicine."

"What kind of doctor are you?"

"The kind that helps people."

"That's what all the doctors here say. They haven't helped me at all."

"What sort of help do you need, Dorothy?"

"I want to leave here."

"For where?"

"Any place."

"Why?"

"Because any place is better than here."

"Perhaps we can make 'here' better for you. That'd be a step in the right direction, don't you think?"

"I'd still want to go. You can't make it that much better."

"If you *could* go, where would you go? I mean if you could go anyplace, where would it be?"

"I don't know."

"Would it be home?"

"You mean Sunbonnet?"

"Where else?"

". . ."

"You're thinking of the 'other place,' aren't you?"

"Yes. I think of it. Even if nobody believes it exists."

"You'd prefer to go back there?"

"Instead of being here?"

"Instead of being back in Sunbonnet."

"Yes."

"After the tornado, when you arrived back home, you told your family and neighbors that you'd returned because *'there's no place like home.'* But you don't feel that way anymore?"

"I never told them that."

"But I thought . . ."

"They weren't listening. *'There's no place like home'* is just what they wanted to hear. So they *said* I said it."

"What did you really say?"

"I said there's no place *that's* home. No place."

"You still feel that way?"

"What do you think, Dr. Evelyn Grace Wilford?"

CHAPTER 3

It seemed nothing but good news at first. Joyful. Even miraculous.

On the fourth morning after the twister, Dorothy Gale was discovered two miles outside Sunbonnet, sleeping, unharmed, among big yellow pumpkins that lay in a tangle of vines on the Pendleton property. The girl's little dog slept beside her. Mrs. Pendleton had been making her way from the house to the barn to milk the cow, when she noticed a heap in the pumpkin patch. It was just before sunrise, and all was draped in purple shadow. Mrs. Pendleton thought at first the heap was a sleeping animal, perhaps a coyote. The woman clapped her hands to alert the animal to her presence, but a girl sat up slowly, stretching her arms as if this were an ordinary morning and she was awakening in her own bed. Her dog leaped into her lap. Mrs. Pendleton dropped her milking bucket and darted across the patch to the girl.

"What in Heavens are you doing out here? Are you all right?" But even as Mrs. Pendleton questioned her, she recognized her. "You're the Gale girl! The whole town's been looking for you."

Dorothy grimaced. "I didn't mean to cause trouble."

Mrs. Pendleton touched the girl's cheek. "Don't worry, dear. Everyone will be so happy you're home."

"Everyone?" Dorothy asked.

"But . . . what are you doing out here? What happened after the twister? Are you all right?" Mrs. Pendleton knelt beside the girl, who was not dressed for a cold morning, but wore only a soiled blue-and-white gingham dress. Making matters worse, she was barefoot. She could have caught her death.

Dorothy pulled her dog tighter to her. "So we *are* in Kansas?"

"Where else would you be?"

The girl hesitated. "Other places."

"Why are you sleeping in my field, Dorothy?"

Dorothy shrugged. "We got so tired walking. Toto and me. I mean, we'd already been walking for days. In the other place. And then more walking when we got back here. Finally we just couldn't take another step. So we stopped in this field last night." She looked past Mrs. Pendleton to the farmhouse. "We didn't see your house. Or the barn. Your lantern must have been off. But we couldn't take one more step. We'd come from so far."

"Where've you been?"

"An enchanted land."

"What land?"

The Gale girl mumbled something unintelligible.

"What did you say?" asked the good woman.

"There were witches there. And talking beasts, flying monkeys, and a wizard. But he turned out to be only an ordinary man."

"Did you say flying monkeys?"

The girl nodded. "And they wore little red hats and match-ing vests."

Mrs. Pendleton didn't follow. She wouldn't be the last citi-zen of Sunbonnet bewildered by Dorothy's ravings. She took hold of the girl's shoulders, held her at arm's length, and stud-ied her face. Dorothy's brown eyes seemed normal. Her color-ing looked good, though it was hard to say for sure in the purple light just before sunrise. Still, what was this gibberish? Was the poor thing delirious? Had she suffered a blow to the head during the twister? Were these symptoms of starvation from her wanderings since the twister? Or fever? No, the girl's forehead felt cool to Mrs. Pendleton's touch. Where *had* Doro-thy been these past four days? But this was no time to press for answers. What mattered most was simply that it was cold out-side. "Let's get you indoors. I'll make you a nice cup of tea."

"Do you have anything for Toto?"

"Your doggie?"

The girl nodded.

"Does he like tea too?"

"No, but I think he's hungry."

"I'm sure we can find something."

"Thank you. And I'm . . . a bit hungry myself."

Mrs. Pendleton helped the girl to her feet. "We're going to take care of everything, Dorothy." She led the girl toward the house. "Your aunt and uncle will be so relieved to know you're safe. We've all been quite worried for you."

★ ★ ★

By mid-morning, Dorothy Gale was reunited with her aunt and uncle at the offices of Dr. Edmund Ward, who was pleased to report that, despite minor evidence of exposure, the girl was in fine health. At least physically. Dorothy's state of mind was another matter. She could recall nothing before the twister and was immersed instead in obvious fantasy. This concerned Dr. Ward. Nonetheless, the good doctor—balding, bespectacled, and in his graying mid-fifties—did not reveal the gravity of his concern until he was alone with Henry and Emily. He'd instructed his nurse to take Dorothy out of the examining room and to his private office for a hot bowl of soup ordered from the Sunbonnet Grill.

"My hope is that, given a little time, Dorothy's mind will clear," Dr. Ward said.

"The girl's mind was never all that clear to begin with," Henry said.

Dr. Ward removed his glasses, a gesture he'd discovered helped to relax patients and family members because it suggested the "examination" was over, and they could engage in easier conversation. However, there was no easing the aging farm couple. Henry and Emily sat tensely beside each other on small chairs against a wall on which hung a large anatomical chart of the human heart, a simple four-chambered pump. "What do you mean by that, Henry?"

Henry scratched his scalp. "The girl always wants to be some other place than where she is. Wherever, whenever. Even on those rare occasions when we give in and take her to wherever it is she wants to go—a picnic at the river or a trip to the county fair or some other such wasteful entertainment—as soon as she gets there, she wants to be someplace else. It grows wearisome."

"Has she ever spoken of this fantastical place before?" Dr. Ward asked. "A road of yellow bricks, a city made of emeralds . . ."

"I never heard talk of it," Henry said. "But I don't pay mind to the details of her fancies." He turned to his wife. "You ever hear her speak of such things?"

Emily shook her head.

It had been a rough time for Emily. These past days, she'd barely allowed herself to hope for good news. When she first saw the girl in the doctor's examining room, she'd broken into tears. In all the years she'd spent married to Henry, Emily had never let him see her cry. This time she couldn't stop it. But neither could she throw her arms around the girl. She feared that to do so would cause both of them to shatter, like the family's heirloom china that lay in pieces among the wreckage of their home. Emily's heart must have shattered anyway when her niece, sitting on the examination table with her dog in her arms, enthusiastically described a flight up through the funnel of the twister to a magical land peopled by witches (some evil, some good), men made of tin or straw, talking animals, flying monkeys, and other wild delusions. Further, she claimed to have returned to Kansas from this fantastical place by knocking her heels together three times and simply wishing it so. And she believed it!

Emily had always known the girl was dreamy and easily distracted, as her schoolteacher described her; but now Emily realized the girl was seriously touched in the head. Who could be blamed at that moment for wondering if it mightn't have been better for Dorothy if she'd not survived the twister?

"Emily," Dr. Ward's voice broke through her racing thoughts. "Did you ever read the child a book with such things in it?"

Emily had never read storybooks to the girl. Everyone knew that such fancies were ungodly. Even dangerous. So she hadn't.

"Do you think Dorothy might have come upon such a fairy tale on her own?" the doctor pressed. "Might she have picked up a book or periodical in your house?"

Impossible. Aside from the Bible and a *Farmer's Almanac*, there was no need to keep books in the home. The town had no bookseller (outside of a few respectable titles such as *Pilgrim's Progress* and biographies of George Washington and other Founding Fathers for sale at the dry goods store). The lending library consisted of a dimly lit room in the loft of a large shed on the school property. It carried no titles that could be deemed blasphemous in their plots, characters, or actions. Children couldn't check out a book unless it was for a specific school assignment. Even this occurred only rarely among the few older students pursuing a junior high school diploma.

Dr. Ward turned to Henry but then thought better of asking if *he* knew where his niece might have come across such a yarn. Indeed, the doctor wondered, only half jokingly, if Henry even knew his niece's name, as the farmer had referred to her only as "the girl" from the moment he and his wife entered his office. During the physical examination, Dr. Ward learned that in Dorothy's fantasy her three traveling companions had yearned for brains, a heart, and courage, but he'd learned nothing from her about what actually mattered. How had she escaped the destruction of the twister? How and where had she survived on her own these past four days? He gained nothing useful from Henry or Emily, whose melancholic attitudes doubtless predated their present misfortunes. So he moved to the door, opened it, and gestured out toward the hall. "Why don't we rejoin Dorothy in my private office? Now that she's had some hot soup, perhaps her mind will be clearer and we'll get some answers." Down the hall, Dorothy looked rejuvenated by the soup, seated with her dog on her lap in Dr. Ward's swivel chair behind his big desk.

Dr. Ward dismissed his nurse. Henry and Emily sat in the upholstered chairs opposite the desk, where patients regularly receive news good or bad. The doctor remained standing beside them. To one observing the room just then it would have appeared all three adults were awaiting a diagnosis from eleven-year-old Dorothy.

In a sense, they were.

* * *

Unfortunately, the girl's mind was no clearer.

Setting her soup spoon on the doctor's desk blotter, Dorothy said: "Glinda is the witch of the South."

"Witch?" Emily managed.

"You're talking nonsense, girl," Henry said.

"But it's true," Dorothy said. "She's the most powerful of the witches, and she's kind to everyone."

"There'll be no talk of witches."

"But I'm telling you what happened."

Henry shot her a look, and she turned away. Emily said nothing, but her eyes welled with tears.

"Dorothy," Dr. Ward said, "don't you understand that there can be no such place? It's impossible."

Dorothy met the doctor's eye. "There *is* such a place. I was surprised myself. I understand why you have doubts. But it's very, very far away. So things there are . . . very, very different."

"What's this place called?" Dr. Ward said.

"There are different lands there, all named for their peoples." Dorothy glanced away, as if suddenly distracted, as if searching for a glimpse of the place in the wood-paneled room.

After a moment, she sighed. "The whole of it, all the lands taken together, is called Oz. It's named for the leader. He's a wizard. Great and powerful. But bad."

"Wizard, witches?" Emily removed a handkerchief from her handbag and dabbed her eyes. "This is sacrilegious talk, Dorothy. You can stop it right now."

"No," Dr. Ward said to the old woman, "let the girl talk. What do you mean this wizard was bad, dear?"

"He's a good man, but he's a bad wizard. He said so himself."

"What makes him bad? Does he do bad things?"

Dorothy thought about it. "I guess so. But the things he does aren't *too* bad. Not like the Wicked Witch. That's not what he meant when he said he was a 'bad' wizard."

"What did he mean?"

"I think he meant he was a bad wizard because he never really was a wizard at all. He's a fake. But he's clever. And powerful enough, in his own way. After all, the whole land *is* named for him."

"Oz," the doctor said.

Dorothy nodded.

It might have gone on like this for hours, as Dorothy lacked for no detail of her hallucinatory world. However, whatever renewed energy the girl gained from her bowl of soup faded quickly. Accordingly, Dr. Ward was about to suggest to Henry and Emily that they take their niece home (which, for now, was a gas-lit corner of their barn, furnished with secondhand donations from neighbors), when Dorothy made a claim that stopped them all.

"I didn't mean to kill the witch," she said.

Dr. Ward looked taken aback. "To . . . what? To kill what?"

A tear slid from one of the girl's eyes. Until now, she had related her entire fantastical narrative as if it had been a walk in the park. "How was I to know that water would *kill* her?"

"Kill who?" Dr. Ward said. "Who, Dorothy?"

"The witch."

Emily put her hand to her mouth. Henry sat up in his chair.

"Did this witch have a name?" Dr. Ward asked.

"Yes, but I don't remember it. Only that she was dressed all in black and was wicked and everyone in the land was afraid of her." Dorothy choked back a sob. "How was I to know?"

Neither Henry nor Emily moved.

"How were you to know what?" Dr. Ward prompted.

"That throwing the bucket of water at her would kill her." Dorothy cried. "How could I know it would *melt* her? Oh, it was terrible. Melting, melting . . ."

Henry stood up, knocking his chair over as he backed away from his niece. "What did you do, girl?"

"I was just trying to help my friends." Toto scrambled to the floor as Dorothy stood too. "The witch was wicked— *wicked*! So I threw water on her, and the horrible old woman melted. I never meant to kill anyone willingly." Dorothy staggered away from the desk, the little dog yapping at her feet. Then she passed out cold.

★ ★ ★

Afterward, Dr. Ward revived Dorothy and urged the Gales to change their plan and deliver the girl to the home of the Reverend and Mrs. Richter so she could recover her strength. He believed that the makeshift hand-me-down encampment that Henry and Emily had assembled in their drafty rodent-infested barn was no place for an exhausted eleven-year-old girl. Nor was the noisy rebuilding of a house likely to contribute to her convalescence. Besides, it was evident to the good doctor that Emily and Henry no longer felt capable or, frankly, comfortable around their niece. They'd been disconcerted by her recollection of a pagan phantasmagoria and seriously shaken by Dorothy's fantasy that she'd killed someone in that strange world. A witch, of all things. The doctor knew of no better place for the recovery of the girl's spirit as well as her body than the home of the childless but kind Reverend and Mrs. Richter.

"I think it best we keep your niece's claim of having melted a wicked witch to ourselves," Dr. Ward suggested before Henry and Emily left for the Richters. "I see no immediate purpose to spreading that detail around just now."

The couple was quick to agree. Dorothy's fantasy seemed not just tawdry but an evil thing beyond their understanding. It was more an issue for the clergy than mere relatives, further reason to deliver the girl and her dog to the Richters, however impatient with church talk and churchgoing and church doings Henry had always been. Henry was now willing to reconsider his skepticism. Or, at least, to pass the problem on to someone else.

"Will you promise to keep that part about killing a witch to yourself for a little while, Dorothy?" Dr. Ward asked. She nodded assent as the Gales departed.

Disturbing as the girl's imaginings were, it all might have passed.

Not without some damage to the Gale girl's reputation. She had been of suspect mental constitution since she started school. "She's dreamy and sensitive," her teacher reported to the Gales. *Dreamy* and *sensitive* were of no use on a farm. And everyone knew that an idle mind is the Devil's playground. Yet for all these warning signs, who would have ever conceived that the girl might not be merely delusional, but had invented her story to cover a darker truth as yet unrevealed?

Ruminating at his desk after the Gale family left his office, Dr. Ward caught sight of a small, wholly unexpected detail across the room. He was looking for no such clue that might suggest any forethought on the girl's part. The full implications would not be immediately apparent. Nonetheless, he found himself disconcerted.

At the time, he still believed the child had experienced shock and was suffering from a disturbing hallucination that would likely pass in short order. The truth of her whereabouts these past days would emerge in time. Besides, irreligiosity was no concern of his. Doctors are trained to think this way. He knew she was troubled, but he did not imagine her to be malevolent.

Perhaps the good doctor should have suspected the girl sooner. But we citizens of Sunbonnet are by nature trusting, being raised on Gospel truths and the Lord's Providential gifts—our fields, our shops, our homes, and one another. We are grateful. That is why when Dr. Ward leaned back in his chair, precisely where Dorothy had sat a half hour before, what he saw shocked him to his soul.

His filing cabinet stood across the room in direct line of sight from the desk.

The cabinet consisted of two drawers that contained the files of all his patients. The top drawer was labeled "A–N."

The second drawer, "O–Z."

This brought Dr. Ward to his feet. "Oz," he said aloud to no one.

He was aghast at the audacity of the girl's invention, the boldness of her imagination, the conviction of her performance, the depth of her perversion. When he'd asked her for the name of her fairyland, mightn't she have merely glanced across the room? Had she taken note of the label on the bottom drawer of the cabinet to concoct a quick answer to his question? O–Z. Oz. Might there be any other explanation? Yes, coincidence. But what were the odds against such a thing? And so, if Dorothy *had* conceived the name in a conscious, purposeful fashion, then mightn't she have concocted the whole story in the same way?

But to what end? Why?

It wouldn't be until the discovery of poor Alvina Clough the next day that Dr. Ward would posit an answer for the girl's seemingly irrational calculation. Even then he would be hard-pressed to believe such corruption possible. Absent news of the murder, he walked to the filing cabinet. O–Z. He did not ask himself if Dorothy might be taking refuge from the consequences of possible misconduct committed during her mysterious absence by thus inviting the lesser consequences of lunacy. He did not ask himself how any mere child could be capable of such duplicity. These questions did not occur to him—not yet. They were still a day away. All the same, he felt a grave disturbance.

Dr. Ward possessed one of the four or five telephones in Sunbonnet still operational after the vehement storm. He went to the wall, picked up the earpiece, cranked the handle on the side of the device, and leaned close to the mouthpiece. After a moment, the connection went through.

"Hello?"

"Reverend Richter?" the doctor inquired.

"Yes?"

"This is Doctor Ward. Is the Gale girl there at your house?"

"Yes. The Gales were just here. Dorothy's having a cup of tea now with the missus."

"There's something more you need to know about the girl," Dr. Ward said, enunciating his words to be understood over the crackling line. "Something you ought to share with your wife."

Dr. Ward told the reverend of Dorothy's murderous confession, along with his reservations regarding the file cabinet as possible evidence of conscious manipulation rather than helpless hallucination on the girl's part. In this light, he cautioned the reverend to pay close attention.

"But why would she choose to concoct such things?" Reverend Richter asked. "To what end?"

"I don't know. But I thought you should be informed."

"I see." The reverend sighed. "Well, to what better place than into the arms of the clergy could such a deeply troubled girl come?"

What followed in the immediate aftermath would strike Sunbonnet more powerfully than any tornado. Immediate word of Dorothy's return from oblivion swept through us with a combination of grateful wonder for the girl's survival and condemnation for her pagan "recollection" of wizards and witches. At first, we were denied the most chilling details of the girl's phantasmagoria, as the reverend had agreed with Dr. Ward to withhold word of Dorothy having *melted* a black-clad, reviled hag. The two men also agreed to keep to themselves the implications of the "O–Z" label on the file cabinet. Good advice, short-lived as it was. Reverend Richter proved more than merely wise but also most Christian in his acceptance of the dread responsibility of bringing Dorothy into their home. The Richter household embraced the dictum *"Hate the sin but love the sinner."* This didn't stop the reverend from locking the girl into the second-story bedroom at night. Devout as he was, he was no reckless fool.

We still had plenty to speculate about that first day of Dorothy's return, even without news of the file cabinet or the *melting*. We debated Dorothy's actual whereabouts during her missing days. How does a girl disappear on the prairie when the whole town is looking for her? And on a more distressing note, we wondered how such impious things as living scarecrows and talking animals could ever have seemed real to the girl, however disorienting her experience of the twister. Such fantasies were discouraged in our community, and for good reason. Decadence. Gaiety. Puerility. But far worse than characters of mere fancy were the wizard and witches in the Gale girl's "reminiscence." We knew our Bible—Leviticus 19:31: *"Regard not them that seek after wizards . . ."* To say nothing of other powerful admonitions found in Isaiah, Deuteronomy, Exodus, and a dozen other places in the Good Book. Still, our concern then for the girl's moral well-being consisted of worry only that her irreligious imaginings might open a doorway to sin sometime in her future; we never suspected she might have already committed a sin of the gravest consequence, the dark sin of Cain. How could we imagine such a thing of a child?

We didn't know yet that a murder had occurred. Such evil lay beyond our imaginations. But not for long.

CHAPTER 4

The handful of doctors' notes detailing their interviews with Dorothy G. are useless to me. The distinguished gentlemen all suffer from the misconception that simply by identifying the girl's malaise as *dementia praecox*, they have provided the patient with actual medical assistance. These august gentlemen note only that the girl has suffered an intense hallucination, specifying little of the hallucination itself, as if its details were of no concern. This attitude is not unique to the doctors here in Kansas. It is pervasive in Harvard's Lawrence Hall too. And Bellevue in New York. It is why I am here now, exposing myself to the dismissive shrugs and disdainful side-glances by which I am often greeted by my so-called colleagues. But that is no matter to me.

Unfortunately, one doctor, whom I shall not deign to name, *did* prescribe further treatment for the girl. In my estimation, it would have been far better had Dorothy G. been medically ignored rather than subjected to such an outdated but still too familiar measure. Stripped by a nurse and plunged into a tub, the girl was deluged by five buckets of ice-cold water poured in succession over her head. After experiencing sensations akin to drowning, she was yanked from the tub, gasping and quaking. The matron pulled a flannel slip labeled "Topeka Insane Asylum" over the girl. In this physician's notes the procedure was described as having failed to return the patient to health, and so a second and then a brutal third treatment were ordered. So long as I am here, I will see that this doesn't happen to her again. But I cannot stay here forever. It worries me greatly that the same cannot be said of Dorothy G.

"Have you come to see others here, Dr. Evelyn Grace Wilford?"

"Just you."

"Why?"

"You're very interesting to me."

"Interesting? That makes me feel like some kind of rare caterpillar."

"I didn't mean it that way."

"Maybe I'm not as interesting as you think. And maybe not everything you read about me in those notes is true."

"Tell me something about yourself others have gotten wrong."

"I'm not a murderess."

"What about the witch? Didn't you melt her?"

"I did. But it's not murder if you didn't mean to kill."

"What about when—"

"I don't want to talk about killing. It never does any good."

"All right. We don't need to talk about it."

"Usually, it's all people want to talk about with me. They pretend to be interested in other things. But they're not. Is that what you're doing, pretending with me?"

"No."

". . ."

"May I remind you, Dorothy, I didn't bring up the matter of killing. You did."

"Well, you've come a long way just to talk to a girl who's crazy."

"Are you crazy?"

"No."

"I think you may be right."

"But aren't you a doctor for people who are crazy?"

"That's not how I'd describe my specialty."

"Then why are you here, Dr. Evelyn Grace Wilford?"

"You don't have to call me by my whole name. You can call me Dr. Wilford."

"Why did you come all this way to see me?"

"I'm interested in your experience of Oz."

"Everyone else calls it my fantasy. Or my dream. Or my brain illness."

"I'm not interested in what others call it, Dorothy."

"You called it my 'experience' of Oz."

"What's wrong with that?"

"An experience is not very different from calling it a fantasy or dream or illness."

"That's not how I meant it. What's a better word I could have used?"

"My *visit*. Just that simple. My visit to Oz."

"Oh, I see. I am interested in your visit to Oz."

"What do you want to know?"

"What's it like there?"

"It's different. Very. I knew that soon as I arrived. Before I even met anyone."

"How did you know?"

"I stepped outside the wreckage of our house and I *saw*. Immediately."

"Saw what?"

"Colors."

"Brighter than here in Kansas?"

"Much brighter than it is in here. There were so many huge flowers and rare birds and a whole city made of emeralds. But I can't say for sure how it compares with Kansas."

"Why not?"

"Because I don't know exactly how colorful Kansas is."

"I don't understand."

"Last year I was tested in school, and my teacher told me I have color blindness. Dr. Ward said so too. It's very rare for girls. I have problems with reds and greens. My yellows aren't so good either. Of course, I didn't know there was anything wrong with me until they told me. And even then it didn't make much difference in my life. You don't know what you can't see if you've never seen it, can you?"

"I guess not."

"But in Oz, I saw colors that *were* red and green. I'm sure of it. The Emerald City is glittering green. The Quadling country is red. I had no trouble telling the difference. The land of the Winkies is yellow, and so is the brick road. I miss all those colors now I'm back in Kansas. Red and green are the same again. Oh, sure, the sky is as blue here as it was there, but everything beneath the sky is drab. It never was before. Kind of sad.

Because now I know what it is I can't see. I miss so many things about Oz. Aside from my scarecrow friend, those colors are what I miss most of all."

"That sounds remarkable."

"It's a remarkable place."

"Tell me about this scarecrow friend of yours."

"He was my first friend there. After the Munchkins. And Glinda. I helped him down from a pole in the middle of a cornfield. And he became my best friend. Although I kept that *best* business to myself. I didn't want to hurt any of my other new friends' feelings."

"That's thoughtful of you. Did this scarecrow have a name?"

"He was just the Scarecrow."

"What other kind of people live in Oz?"

"I wouldn't call them people. Not all of them. I mean, some were talking animals, and some were made of straw or tin or china or, in the case of the witch, dust. At least, I think she was made of dust. You couldn't tell by looking at her. She looked like an ordinary woman except for her greenish skin, her black gown, and peaked cap. But she wasn't ordinary. If she'd been made of normal flesh and blood, she wouldn't have melted like she did when I accidentally splashed her with a bucket of water. Anyway, they weren't any of them regular people. Or . . ."

"Or what?"

"I don't know. Maybe everybody's right."

"About what?"

"Maybe none of it was real."

" . . ."

"Being here has made me begin to doubt myself, Dr. Evelyn Grace Wilford."

"I have no doubt it was real to you."

"I never lied about it, if that's what you mean."

"Would you like to tell me more about your friends?"

"Well, there was the Cowardly Lion and the Tin Man and
many others, but . . .

"But what?"

"Do I have to talk about them right now? It makes me miss
them."

"You can talk about whatever you'd like."

". . ."

"What would you like to talk about, Dorothy?"

"New York is very far away."

"It is."

"How did you hear about this? About me?"

"My cousin is a newspaper reporter in Chicago. He came
to Sunbonnet to write a story about all the goings-on
after the tornado."

"You mean to write about the murder and . . . me."

"Even when he finished his story, he still had lots of questions. He asked the townsfolk, but he didn't get many
answers. He thinks the world of you, Dorothy. And he's
worried about your being here. He couldn't see any
way to help you since he has no training as a doctor. So
he wrote to me because he thought I'd be interested.
And he was right."

"There's that word interested again.

"You're not an exotic caterpillar to me."

"Then why did your cousin think you'd be interested in
me?"

"I'll tell you why. I take very seriously the stories, recollections, and impressions that people relate. I take them seriously even when others don't. *Particularly* when others don't. Because I believe there's always some kind of truth in them."

"What if someone's just lying?"

"Are you lying, Dorothy?"

"Everyone tells me my recollections are nonsense. They just want me to get over them."

"I believe they're the ones talking nonsense."

"So you *don't* want me to get over them?"

"'Getting over' them is not the point."

"Then what is?"

"Nothing so simple as that."

"But . . . if I *did* get over them would they let me out of here?"

"Unfortunately, that's not so simple either."

"So, if it doesn't matter one way or the other, why do you care what I remember?"

"Your recollections are valuable for their own sake."

"Valuable to who?"

"You."

"And to you too, Dr. Evelyn Grace Wilford?"

"Absolutely."

"Why?"

"Because I want to learn how to listen in a new way that might help me to better understand people."

"Do you have a problem understanding others?"

"We all do."

"But do you have a particular problem?"

"I didn't come here to talk about myself."

"Do you work with other crazy children?"

"Actually, I've never worked with a child before. And I
    thought we agreed you aren't crazy."

"*I'm* agreed I'm not crazy. But you're an awful doctor if you
    already agree."

"Why's that?"

"I haven't proven anything to you yet."

"We have time."

"If you're interested in Oz . . . well, you didn't have to come
    all this way. Most of it's written down in the other doc-
    tors' notes. You could have saved yourself a long, dusty
    train ride."

"I read their notes. I don't think they know what to make of
    your story. How to appreciate it, how to hear it at all.
    That's why it's not enough for me to simply read about
    their understanding of Oz. I wanted to talk about it
    with you. And about you. Is that all right?"

"I guess so."

"Before we start, let me ask you something: What's the
    worst thing about being here for you?"

". . ."

"I'd like to know if I can help you in some practical way. Is
    there something you need?"

"The worst is the loneliness."

". . ."

"The nurses don't talk to me. Just order me around. And
    the other ladies who I sometimes see in the dining hall
    or on the grounds . . . are much older than me. All
    grown up. And they're here because they suffer from
    what's called nervous debility. They're always talking
    to invisible friends or enemies, laughing or crying.

They scare me even when they take an interest in me or try to be nice. Actually, when they're friendly is the scariest of all. And I can tell I scare some of them too. They've heard stories about me. So I keep a distance. I miss Toto most."

"Your dog?"

"Yes. Even when I was captive of the Wicked Witch, she didn't take Toto. And she was wicked through and through. Will I ever see Toto again?"

"I'll look into it. Perhaps I can help. Anything else?"

"It's very hard to sleep. All night long one nurse or another marches up and down the halls. And then every half hour they rattle their keys in the lock of my door and open it with a terrible loud creaking to check if I'm sleeping. Which I'm not because their marching and snooping, and snooping and marching, has kept me awake. I hate them for ruining my sleep. Maybe more than anything else because it keeps me from dreaming. And that's the only way I have of escaping this place."

CHAPTER 5

The body belonged to Alvina Clough, a spinster of fifty-one, who lived alone in the three-story house her long-dead father had built when he founded our upstanding prairie town forty years ago. The twister had only touched down here and there in Sunbonnet proper. Besides knocking out many of the newly installed electrical and telephone lines, it did little damage. Still, the great gusts of wind proved powerful enough to wrench a shutter off the ground floor of Alvina's house. Ripped from its hinges, the shutter hurtled about the porch before whipping through the front window, shearing the blue velvet draperies that kept both daylight and prying eyes from penetrating her inner sanctum. Alvina's six-foot-tall hedge, which ran along the boundary of her property, was thick enough that we couldn't see through to the house, even if we'd been alerted to the damage. Further, Alvina's absence in town in the days following the twister was no indication that anything unusual had occurred. After all, she rarely left her home (even for Sunday church services), and as she had no family or friends to speak of, she was not immediately missed. We were distracted just then by other matters. The Gale girl's disappearance, for example. Our neighborly goodwill had been pressed to near capacity by the daily search parties to find the girl's remains. We couldn't know that Dorothy would turn up of her own account, healthy of body in a pumpkin patch. Many of us had suffered damage on our own properties, and the sounds of hammers and saws were near continuous. If truth be told, distraction was not the whole of our reluctance to call at Alvina's house after the storm. The four-day period between the shutter slamming through her window and us eventually inquiring after her health can best be understood by describing the woman herself.

This was Alvina Clough: The town's most prickly citizen.

To those of us who'd grown up in Sunbonnet, she seemed to be less a human being subject to the ordinary passage of time than an immutable element of nature. She was a misshapen and craggy peak on our otherwise flat prairie land. This may seem a coarse appraisal of a pitiable woman, but Alvina had acted wretched, hostile, and old beyond her years for as long as any of us could remember. These characteristics isolated her; the sternness of her bun and the black umbrella she carried with her at all times afforded her unique power among us, power even beyond her wealth. Alvina cared not a whit for our welfare or opinions, and so she never allowed for any way but her own. She disdained the social consolations we treasured—community, church, courtship, marriage, children. All that mattered to her was that she be free from all consideration for others. It was only natural that in time we felt free of consideration for her. Admittedly, this was not a very Christian attitude; but who among us is not a sinner? Since we paid Alvina so little mind, nothing ever seemed to change in her life. From our perspective, one month, one year, one decade of her life seemed the same as any other.

Still, when it came to her, we weren't heartless.

More than one generation of parents in our town had lectured, threatened, and punished their children for calling Alvina a witch, even though they'd called her a witch when they themselves were young. Some good-hearted townswomen had tried to befriend her on three separate occasions over the past twenty years: Margaret Ryan, our old postmaster's wife; Dr. Ward's now-deceased wife, Gladys; and Elizabeth Richter, the reverend's wife, had all invited her to join them for an event.

The first, twenty years ago, was for an ice cream social; then nine years later for a church picnic; and finally, three years ago, for a piano recital. Alvina accepted the invitations and arrived to well wishes. In each instance—before the ice cream started to melt, before the first ear of corn was slathered in butter, before the visiting pianist played a single note—Alvina opened the gloomy doctor's bag she carried in lieu of a reticule. She then withdrew a pile of threatening legal papers that she passed on to several unfortunates among the socializing ladies. Not very neighborly . . .

During the ice cream social, she passed around to nine redfaced women notarized documents demanding immediate unpaid interest on personal loans their families had privately secured through Alvina. She often served as banker to the less financially established among us, specifically when First Kansas proved unwilling to risk such a loan. At the church picnic she doled out three court summonses to neighbor women whose houses failed to meet the ordinances Alvina's father had established when he founded our town. Finally, she cast an irrevocable pall over the piano recital by delivering foreclosure notices to two mortified farm wives. (Alvina personally secured private mortgages as well.) After that, even the most open-hearted ladies and their organizations concluded once and for all that Alvina would never change. Alvina didn't seem to mind. Being left alone may have been her intention all along.

What had happened to make her this way in the first place? We never knew. We still don't know. We never will. But we knew this: stepping up to knock on Alvina's door was an invitation to derision. That's why it took us longer than might be thought proper to get around to it.

Nevertheless, we did it.

One day after Dorothy's baffling return to our town, we stepped up to Alvina's door to knock, ready to help her in any way necessary.

Sheriff Hutchins led our small group onto the porch.

There was no answer at the door, so we moved to the broken front window and peered in.

"Miss Clough?" the sheriff called into the house.

No answer.

Sheriff Hutchins glanced back at us before climbing through the broken window, gesturing for us to follow. Once inside, we stepped over the shutter that had crashed through the glass. We picked our way around a scattering of glass shards large enough to cut a man's throat. Most of us had never set foot inside Alvina's house. The room was crammed with ornate furnishings and Persian rugs, which came as no surprise considering what we believed then was Alvina's wealth. However, we were most taken aback by the curios and souvenirs from Europe displayed about the room. Brass castings of the Roman Coliseum, the Tower Bridge in London, and Notre Dame Cathedral in Paris, all small enough to hold in one hand. Lace doilies dyed in the colors of national flags.

Over a decade ago, Alvina had taken a yearlong tour of the continent. No one from Sunbonnet had indulged in such a voyage before. It was the only time Alvina left our town for more than a day or so. Never being the chatty sort, she shared no recollections from her Grand Tour. She returned with a trunk full of souvenirs and doled them out with uncharacteristic enthusiasm to a number of townspeople. It was the only neighborly thing she did in her life, as far as any of us could remember. We didn't know until we climbed through her window that her own parlor was crowded with the very same curios that here and there decorated our own homes. It was almost enough to make us see her in a different light.

"Miss Clough? It's Sheriff Hutchins. Are you here?" We continued through the front parlor and toward the hall. "Alvina?" he called. "Are you all right?"

Something smelled rotten. The Sheriff pointed past the staircase and back toward the kitchen.

It was the stink of decaying flesh. Along with a sharp odor of something else—a pungent chemical stench. We hoped it was a rotting raccoon or cat that had gotten in through the open window and partaken of the rat poison that Alvina placed like Christmas candy in fine bone china saucers at precise six-foot intervals along the floorboards of her curio-crowded rooms.

We followed the sheriff into the kitchen.

It wasn't a raccoon or cat we smelled.

At her kitchen table, the remains of Alvina Clough sat upright in a straight-back chair, almost as if she'd just set down the empty teacup on the dainty saucer before her. There was dried white froth about her mouth and nose, and her tongue hung from her slack mouth. Much of her scalp and face seemed to drip like putrid wax down her right shoulder and into the lap of her black dress. Her right cheekbone gleamed a bright white where the flesh had been. Her right eyeball was milky and sightless in its socket. The forehead and scalp had come away from the exposed skull, leaving strands of coarse black hair among the fleshy drippings in her lap. Some among us were forced to turn away. A few silently moved back through the kitchen to vomit in the yard. We are not generally a squeamish lot. Being members of a farming community, we've been exposed to nature's vagaries and violence. Calves are sometimes born with two heads. Coyotes tear unfortunate lambs to bits and leave their snowy fleece scattered on farmers' porches like winter dustings. Animals of all sorts are routinely taken from family pens and slaughtered. It is our business. Our way of life. The prairie is hard. But a woman's head melted away?

The sheriff was among those who excused themselves to the yard. We didn't think less of him. At least, not much less.

After the initial shock, those of us who remained in the kitchen glanced from the body to one another, then back to the body. Finally, we turned our attention to the room itself. We took in the scene less as an investigative act and more as a distraction from the gruesome remains at the kitchen table. No one made a move toward Alvina. Handkerchiefs clasped over our noses, we breathed shallowly to avert nausea. Almost as one, we retreated to where the smell was bearable enough that we could lower our handkerchiefs and absorb this horrific sight.

"What happened to her? What in God's name happened!"

"Her face is melted."

"Lye?"

"No, it's the truth, for God's sake."

"I mean lye, the chemical. You can smell it."

"Oh. Right."

"Somebody *did* this to her?"

"It's not the kind of thing someone could do to herself. Even the most miserable suicide would use rat poison before she'd . . ."

"Burn her face off?"

"Alvina's been murdered?"

It's important to note that we who'd gathered in Alvina's house had not yet learned of Dorothy Gale's claim to have "melted" a witch. So far, we'd heard only the disturbing satanic generalities of the girl's strange fantasia—not her claim of killing. Had we known, we likely would have discovered our capacities for horror pressed beyond the breaking point. Even more disturbing than an old woman slain by a cruel method, leaving behind a corpse worthy of the perverse writer Edgar Allan Poe, is an eleven-year-old girl capable of committing such an offense.

We didn't yet know enough to be plagued by such a question. Our horror was still of the *nearly* overwhelming variety.

"Who would do such a thing to a poor old woman?" someone whispered as we made our way out of that hellish kitchen.

★ ★ ★

Our natural impulse was to immediately vacate the noxious premises. But we remained in the front hallway, held by an unspoken need to compose ourselves before we emerged onto the clean, sunlit streets of our town. Alvina had been brutally murdered. That was a fact. What were we to make of the unprecedented calamity? What were we to say to others? How were we to return to our children and offer them the comforts of Proverbs 3:29: *"Do not plan evil against your neighbor, who dwells trustingly beside you"*? We'd just gained the painful but indisputable knowledge that at least one *un*trustworthy neighbor dwelt among us. We hesitated in the hallway, out of our depths but at least together.

"This is terrible," said Humphreys, the druggist, wiping furiously at his eyes as if to clear them of what he had just seen. "What are we going to do?"

"*You* got to do something," said Garrison, the general store manager.

"Why me?" asked Humphreys.

"Because you're a medical man," Wilson the blacksmith insisted.

"I'm not the *doctor* in this town," the druggist snapped. "All I do is mix up poultices."

"That's right," said Garrison. "That's why we've got to get the doctor."

Humphreys nodded. "He'll know what to do."

"Alvina doesn't need a doctor," observed Patterson, the dapper bachelor who managed the Peabody Hotel. "She's beyond medical attention. Somebody's got to go for the reverend."

"She don't need the reverend any more than she needs a doctor," Wilson said.

We turned to Wilson with startled expressions. Under what circumstances was a pious man of the cloth unnecessary? Was the smithy being as disrespectful and ungodly as Henry Gale had been the morning after the twister?

"What I mean," Wilson spluttered, shaken by our unease, "is that Alvina's soul is already among the angels . . . Or . . . in the other place? Whichever place is appropriate. Probably, the other place since it's Alvina we're talking about."

The slightly built druggist looked the burly blacksmith in the face. "There's no call to be disrespectful of the departed, Mr. Wilson. Besides, it's sacrilegious to speculate about damnation."

"Stop sniping," snapped Patterson, the hotel man. "What Alvina needs is the undertaker. This is *his* job. Not ours. All we got to do is let him know what's happened."

"No, gentlemen," said Sheriff Hutchins, returning to the front hallway from outside. "It's not that simple." He looked at us as if we'd proven a disappointment to him. "Are you some sort of useless lot?"

We were happy to let the sheriff claim command of the moment. Responsibility for it too. It was his job, after all.

"I overheard your discussion of proper procedure," the sheriff continued. "I'm surprised one of you didn't suggest fetching the florist to put together a nice corsage to complement poor Alvina's outfit." Ordinarily, the sheriff wasn't one for sarcasm, but we didn't object to it now. We thought it likely he was still embarrassed by his bolting from the kitchen to vomit.

"We were just taking poor Alvina into account," the blacksmith said. "Her earthly remains and all. Out of respect. What to do for her."

"She's dead, Wilson," the sheriff said. "So the best thing we can do for the poor woman is figure out who killed her. Obviously, none of you has any experience with this kind of thing."

"True." But neither had he.

Ours was not a crime-ridden community. Oh, there'd been fistfights over the years at one or the other of our two saloons; some of the fights had grown sufficiently violent as to include the uses of knives; broken bottles; and, once, a gun. Men had been wounded, scarred, and jailed, but none had been killed ever. Fighting was just what men did. A rite of passage. After all, nobody wants a generation of weak-kneed, anemic young-sters working the livestock or tilling the fields.

There *had* been a murder in the next town a decade before. A farmer named Olson took offense at a neighbor's immoral dalliance with Olson's daughter and had beaten the neighbor to death with a shovel. Olson was convicted and imprisoned for one year, spared from hanging because the crime was adjudged to have been partially justified. In any case, we were farmers, shopkeepers, and respectable tradesmen. Nonetheless, there *was* a killer, apparently stealthy and cruel.

And there was a sheriff. "Gentlemen, you all go for the undertaker," he instructed. "He'll transport the body. And while you're at it, send Deputy Cutter. Tell him to bring a couple of lanterns, since he and I may be here well into the night. Advise him not to eat anything before he comes over because . . . well, I guess I don't have to explain to you. I'll take charge of things here. You can go now."

But we didn't go. Not immediately. We glanced back at the kitchen, hesitating but not speaking. The moment kept coming on at us.

Murder.

Despite Alvina's aversion to it, there'd be a church service. Then she'd be buried in the churchyard plot beside her mother, father, and a twin sister who'd died as a child. Later in the week there'd be a reading of her will. As none of us expected to be bequeathed so much as a penny, we hadn't much interest in that. Still, standing in her grand house, we couldn't help wondering: Who *would* inherit her fortune?

"Get on with yourselves," Sheriff Hutchins rasped, rousing us from our strange spell—the spell of death in the next room.

And then we were out of Alvina's house forever.

★ ★ ★

There's a limit to the amount of disturbing news townsfolk can absorb in any given week before disquiet seeps into our waking minds. We were nearing that density. First, the tornado and then the disappearance of the Gale girl and her mysterious reappearance. Second, the murder of Alvina Clough, who for years had been considered the worst person living in our town. Her death now served as irrefutable evidence that there was one among us far more malicious than Alvina had ever been. Taken together, this tested our mettle. But life on the prairie made us strong. We'd have endured it all with little more than a sharing of anxious words among the farm wives at the dry goods store or a lengthening of the ordinary silences among the working men during breaks at the granary. Doubtless, there'd be pointed Bible verses from the reverend. Something to reassure our sense of justice, such as Leviticus 24:17: *"If a man takes the life of any human being, he shall surely be put to death."* Or something instructive to our own place in such drama, such as Proverbs 28:17: *"A man who is laden with the guilt of human blood will be a fugitive until death; let no one support him."*

Oh, we'd pause a moment longer than usual and tip our hats in the street to Sheriff Hutchins, knowing he was investigating the case. But *our* lives would remain steady. And when we learned that the two events—the disappearance of the Gale girl and the murder of Alvina Clough—converged in a manner we'd never have imagined, we were forced to reconsider who we were. After all, if an eleven-year-old girl could be a cold-blooded murderess . . .

Was it possible that Reverend Richter—even at his fire-and-brimstone best—had actually *underestimated* how far from grace Man had fallen?

★   ★   ★

News of the sort that Doctor Ward, Reverend Richter, and Emily and Henry Gale kept from us is as slippery to hold as a freshly caught fish. Less than two days after Alvina's body was discovered, we were discussing the shocking and terrible implications of Dorothy Gale's confession that she had "melted" a "witch," an unmistakable reference to Alvina Clough. We also speculated about the girl's plunder of the initials on the bottom drawer of Dr. Ward's file cabinet to give her damnable fantasy world a name. Who was it that first broke confidence with the doctor, reverend, and relatives to share the information with us? Since most of us came upon it secondhand, or even third, we couldn't say with certainty. But the source of the disclosure didn't matter. The news itself did. The sheriff warned us against jumping to conclusions, and we nodded solemnly at his admonitions, but we didn't feel we were jumping at anything. We were merely putting two and two together.

When we added it up, we came to an even more vexing question: Why would the Gale girl have incorporated into her fantastical yarn disconcerting details that echoed Alvina's brutal murder? Doing so risked throwing light upon the very thing her wild story seemed concocted to conceal. Was she boasting of her actions? This was the only answer that made sense to us. But what a horrific possibility. What kind of child *was* this?

Naturally, we were mortified. If such things could happen in a town like ours, was it any wonder the world outside was a catastrophe? And trepidation was not all we felt. We were engrossed by the drama of it. The sinfulness. We harkened back to the day after the twister, when we mounted that search party for Dorothy—through the sorghum, past the watering hole, on to the road—and we reflected upon Henry Gale's disrespectful attitude toward Reverend Richter and the gospel truths offered that day. Henry had ridiculed the very notion of the Lord's grace when the reverend suggested it as consolation. His lack of concern about his niece's well-being struck us then and afterward as unfeeling and irresponsible, but not downright evil, like his dismissal of a man of the cloth. We couldn't help but speculate that Henry's skeptical attitudes must have infected his niece, and so we were doubly grateful that the girl was still locked in the Richters' upstairs bedroom.

Many among us shared long-withheld reservations about the Gales. This was no ordinary farm family. How had we never acknowledged that fact publicly before? Now, in the newly somber light that illuminated Sunbonnet, we began our reconsideration with a summary of what little we knew about Dorothy's origins.

We knew the girl was an orphan, her father being Henry Gale's nephew. Long childless, middle-aged Henry and Emily had adopted Dorothy after the parents were killed in a railroad accident. Or was it a boating accident? Or a flood? Or a fire? The details were vague—and no one volunteered to ask Henry or Emily, who had taken to their barn for privacy, doubtless born of shame. In any case, Dorothy's parents died when she was only a few months old, so she had no memory of them. Neither Henry nor Emily ever talked about the deceased relations. On the prairie we don't press folk for information. Our community is tightly knit, but many among us prefer to keep themselves to themselves, and we do not hold it against them.

City folk are the talkers, ever anxious to reveal their thoughts to anyone and his brother who has a moment to listen. We appreciate quiet here. We respect it. We are part of the quiet. But in the case of the Gale family, we may have allowed that respect to diminish our proper neighborly vigilance. I suppose that's obvious now—but it only became obvious *after* the crime.

Once again, who among us could have imagined such a thing?

Gathered in the general store, the saloon, the cigar stand, and our own homes, we agreed upon the following as facts:

Henry and Emily had arrived in Sunbonnet from Missouri fifteen years earlier. They'd been farmers there, but drought had driven them away. The Gales did not socialize; nonetheless, we considered them God-fearing if by no means devout. When the infant girl came into their lives, we were gratified that they raised her as their own and overjoyed when they started showing up at Sunday service from time to time (enough at least to avoid the reverend's cautionary words and sneering glances from the town ladies).

Henry worked hard on his farm, though he never managed to get much ahead. Emily baked the requisite number of pies for church socials and civic functions. Dorothy attended school with the other town children, excelling at spelling and reading while fumbling slightly at arithmetic and geography. The girl had few close friends, though that likely owed more to the long stretches when Henry and Emily kept her home to help with chores than it did with an inability to befriend other children. Indeed, in the schoolyard, she organized many make-believe games with other girls—a chilling thought, now. As previously noted, her teacher, Mrs. Franklin, thought her "dreamy." Even after the murder, we didn't blame Mrs. Franklin for failing to recognize Dorothy's distractibility or her playground fantasies as something that only comes about from an idle and dangerous mind. We didn't blame Mrs. Franklin for any of it, but we did agree that perhaps it was time she considered retirement.

Although the sheriff shared details of the murder investigation only with Mayor Watt-Smith and Reverend Richter, a few tidbits slipped out. For example, we learned that when confronted with the crime, Dorothy vehemently denied it. "It was the Wicked Witch I melted, not Miss Clough," she said. When further pressed, however, she could offer no explanation for her whereabouts during the critical days and nights when the murder must have taken place. Instead, she claimed to have no recollection of anything that happened between the first appearance of the twister on the horizon and her awakening with her dog in the Pendletons' pumpkin patch.

Dorothy claimed to remember nothing—nothing but her time in the land of Oz. She clung so desperately to her story that the more impressionable among us briefly wondered if the damnable lie could be real.

Chapter 6

Upon calling again on Dorothy G., I was asked by the head nurse to wait in the women's recreation room. This space and the entertainments contained therein are offered to lesser afflicted patients as rewards for good behavior. Large windows, barred for safety, overlook the grounds. The natural light here is good. For that reason, this is the room that hospital staff most often shows to visiting administrators or dignitaries. Two card tables are set at either end of the room, though women aren't allowed playing cards due to their "inherent immoral character" (the cards, not the women). Numerous pieces from incomplete wooden jigsaw puzzles litter the tables. These pieces are sometimes shuffled about but rarely fitted together. A pair of worn velveteen sofas mirror each other in the center of the room, and a piano stands near the door. I am told the instrument gets well used; for whatever reason, a high percentage of patients know how to play. Music is said to "soothe the savage beast." But if that is so, why do so many mental patients play? A research project for an undergraduate perhaps. Not for me. Regardless, the playing is useful, as other women, some of whom may not otherwise speak aloud, often sing along. Music may be the only pleasure available here. Surely the food, clothing, accommodations, activities, and companionship offer precious little pleasure.

When not singing, the poor creatures chatter to themselves or engage in passionate arguments with invisible worlds. One patient observed me taking in the scene and nudged me. Sagely nodding her head, she advised me to pay no attention to them "since they're all mad." She then claimed to be the institution's head doctor, all along keeping her arms wrapped tightly around her body as if constrained by an imaginary straitjacket.

Despite my training, I confess to breathing a sigh of relief when the head nurse fetched me away to the empty dining hall where Dorothy awaited.

"Do you work in a hospital, Dr. Evelyn Grace Wilford?

"No. Although I often visit them. I work in a laboratory. The first of its kind in America. We do various tests on many different people."

"Do you take their blood?"

"No, not those kinds of tests. Mostly we ask people lots of questions."

"Do you make up the questions?"

"Sometimes. Maybe not quite as often as I'd like."

"Why not?"

"Well, I'm just now completing my studies at the lab."

"Studies? You have a teacher? But you're a grown-up."

"Yes, I am. Still, I study with a kind and insightful teacher who's very well respected."

"Why?"

"Because he believes that by examining our own thoughts in original and careful ways, we can better understand them. And when we better understand our thoughts, we better understand ourselves. It's rather a new idea."

"Thinking about our own thoughts?"

"Yes. With the help of a doctor. Like my professor—Dr. James."

"What's so good about understanding ourselves?"

"It helps us understand why we do the things we do or don't do."

"What if we already understand why we do things?"

"Most people don't."

"What if I do?"

"Maybe you do. Dr. James believes that even thinking about your own thoughts may help you to understand the world. How you live in it."

"How I live? Like everybody else, I guess."

"Do you really think you're like everybody else?"

"What if I don't want to be like everybody else? What if I can't be like them even if I wish I could?"

"As far as I'm concerned you don't have to be like anyone other than yourself."

". . ."

"Changing who you are is not the point, Dorothy. There doesn't have to be a point to our visiting together at all. Still, there may be something useful to be learned about being yourself. Useful for helping you to live happily in the world as it is."

"Happily? You see this place, how can anyone be happy here?"

"Improvements can be made. Improvements *must* be made. I'll do what I can. I promise. But in the meantime . . ."

"I'm not just talking about this place."

"What do you mean?"

"I'm talking about out there."

"Kansas? I've seen that too, Dorothy."

"I thought you said you just got here."

"Yes, but my first impression of the place is that—"

"I don't understand what you're aiming at with all this talk, Dr. Evelyn Grace Wilford. What are you really here for? To learn something by talking to me? Like the others with their boring, boring, boring questions? Or are you here to teach me something? What do you want me to learn? Why don't you just tell me?"

"This isn't school. Whatever you learn won't come from me, but from you."

"How? Don't I already know what I know?"

"Maybe not. And that's what I'm here to help you find out."

" . . ."

"You're a very clever girl, Dorothy."

"Being clever's not always smart."

"True. But don't you think it would be good to understand your place in the world a little better?"

"There *is* more than one world, Dr. Evelyn Grace Wilford."

"Are you talking about Oz?"

"I'm talking about one world for you and one world for me and as many other worlds as there are other people. And all those worlds are changing all the time. So how can anybody ever hope to keep up?"

"I couldn't have put it better myself, Dorothy. I think you have an excellent grasp of this. A natural understanding."

"Do I? I don't have the faintest idea what we're talking about."

". . ."

"What's so funny?"

"I'm not sure I have the faintest idea what I'm talking about either."

"You're a strange doctor. Other doctors have measured my head, my eyes, nose, lips, chin, ears. Bumps on my skull. They told me it was scientific and would help them understand my mind. Why don't you just do something like that and get it over with?"

"I have all that information already. Here in this file."

"Have you looked at the measurements?"

"I have."

"What do they mean?"

"As far as I'm concerned—nothing. I don't believe in phrenology."

"What's that?"

"Phrenology is the science of measuring heads. Some doctors believe in it. I don't."

"What do you believe in? Your teacher, Professor James?"

"I do believe in that good man. Even if . . ."

"If what?"

"He's an inspiration to me. But I have a few ideas of my own. New approaches. Techniques I'd like to explore."

"Instead of just thinking about thoughts, you mean?"

"Not instead of, but in *addition* to thinking about them."

"What are these techniques, Dr. Evelyn Grace Wilford?"

"I'll show you. I have some new analytical tools here in my bag. Well, old tools actually, but put to a fresh purpose."

". . ."

"Have you ever seen cards like these before, Dorothy?"

"Are they playing cards? We're not allowed playing cards here."

"It's how they were originally used over five hundred years ago. They're still commonly used in some countries for games. But in the centuries since their introduction, they've been put to other uses too."

"Are those the kind of cards used for fortune-telling?"

"Sometimes they're used that way. They're Tarot cards. They were developed in Medieval Europe and—what's wrong?"

"You're trying to get me in trouble—trying to prove something against me. Like everyone else is. Fortune-telling is diabolical. Everyone knows that."

"Please sit back down."

"No! I'm not like they say I am. A child of the devil and all that."

"I know you're not. Don't worry. I didn't bring these cards for fortune-telling."

". . ."

"Like you, Dorothy, I don't believe in fortune-telling. I'm a doctor. A scientist."

"The reverend says a scientist isn't much better than a fortune-teller."

"I won't make you do anything you don't feel right about. Nothing your reverend would disapprove of. I promise."

". . ."

"Thank you, Dorothy."

"I've seen cards like these before. Not up close."

"When?"

"A few years ago, a soothsayer came to our town. Do you know what a soothsayer is?"

"Yes. Tell me about him."

"He drove a horse and a big wagon, and he called himself
Professor Something-or-other. I can't remember. His
name was painted in bright colors on the side of his
wagon, with a beautiful hand. I was only six or seven,
so I couldn't read cursive yet. He used his wagon for
what he called his 'readings.' Everyone knew there was
something different about him. Not necessarily bad.
More like he'd visited faraway countries and met all the
crowned heads. That kind of different. Even us kids
knew it. But then he was gone, and we all knew what
happened to him. It was no secret."

"What happened?"

"He used cards. Like these, I think. For fortune-telling. And
he had a big crystal ball. Some of the ladies went out
to the crossroads to see him. But Reverend Richter
wasn't having any fiendish practices taking place in
Sunbonnet. He spoke out against it. So the men did
things to the soothsayer."

"What did they do?"

"They beat him pretty bad and chased him away. Most
folk said he got off lucky. Naturally he's never come
back."

"That's frightening."

"He was some kind of necromancer. Or so the men said.
He didn't get anything he didn't deserve. They said
that too."

". . ."

"Anyway, these cards are pretty."

"They look familiar to you?"

"I spied on the soothsayer and his lady visitors. He was lay-
ing out cards on a dainty table outside his wagon. They
weren't ordinary playing cards, but had colorful pictures like these. I never saw the cards up close, so I
can't say for sure they were the same as these."

"You spied on him?"

"I climbed a tree and watched him from across the clear-
ing. He wore a strange hat that looked like bandages
wrapped around his head as he dealt out his cards."

"Did you talk to him?"

"No. And I didn't try to sneak inside his wagon. Even when
he was away from it. I'm not crazy. No matter what
people are saying."

"I thought we were agreed you aren't crazy."

"I still haven't proven that to you, Dr. Evelyn Grace Wilford.
If we're not using these cards for fortune-telling and
we're not going to use them to play a game, what are
we doing with them? Why are you showing them to
me? Just for the pretty pictures?"

"Actually, that's not far from the truth. We're going to look
at the pictures together, though not all of them are
pretty."

"Like that one."

"Yes, Dorothy. That's the Death card."

CHAPTER 7

Alvina's funeral was a great success. Reverend Richter delivered an inspirational sermon, one of his best. He quoted Psalms 25:16: *"Turn to me and be gracious to me, for I am lonely and afflicted."* In life, Alvina had given us no good reason to think her either lonely or afflicted. Surely, she was alone and afflict*ing*. That's different. To be lonely, one has to crave human companionship in the first place. To be afflicted, one has to possess normal human vulnerabilities. But now that Alvina was dead, we regarded her differently. The judgment of the Lord was already upon her, so we released our petty judgments and acknowledged that a neighbor most of us had known was gone. Murdered. Yes, we were shaken.

Take Mrs. Humphreys, the druggist's wife. She claimed that the night after the twister, she'd glanced out her second-story window. She was shocked to see Alvina's disembodied spirit floating half a foot above the hard dirt of Main Street. Donned in black from head to toe (as always), Alvina's spirit glided to the door of the church, knelt before it, and then withdrew, disappearing into the darkness. Naturally, Mrs. Humphreys had thought it merely a dream until the body was found two days later. Whenever Mrs. Humphreys related this story, we expressed sadness or deep concern rather than suggesting the obvious—the spirit's inability to *enter* the church indicated Alvina's damnation. We all thought it, though no one spoke the words, out of respect. This charity continued throughout the funeral service. More than one woman among the congregation shed tears for poor Alvina.

The reverend's wife, who possesses a lovely voice, sang "Amazing Grace," accompanied on the organ by the blacksmith's daughter Betsy, a pious dark-haired girl who attended school with Dorothy Gale. To those of us in the pews, Betsy was reassurance that our children had not been tainted by associating with Dorothy.

Ashes to ashes. The ill-tempered but unfortunate Alvina Clough was laid to rest. But not her murder investigation, which proceeded swiftly, as justice ought.

★   ★   ★

Just three weeks after Dorothy and her dog inexplicably turned up in Mrs. Pendleton's pumpkin patch, a circuit judge from Lawrence arrived in Sunbonnet to oversee her case. Sheriff Hutchins reported that he had gathered strong evidence against the girl. Even so, most of us were uncomfortable with the idea of an actual trial for an eleven-year-old, however heinous the crime or unholy her alibi. Fortunately, the judge assigned to the case, Robert Barnhardt Jr., called for a public pretrial hearing. Such a hearing would permit an airing of evidence without requiring a legal verdict, affording flexibility in regard to both plea and sentencing. We agreed that it was the most humane approach to the problem.

The church hall was turned into a makeshift courtroom.

The morning of the hearing, we arrived in numbers great enough to occupy all two hundred seats. The hall ordinarily filled to capacity only for Christmas and Easter pageants. Among us townsfolk were scattered a few out-of-town newspaper reporters drawn to the proceedings by the violence of the murder and how strange it was that a child was the sole suspect. One reporter had come all the way from Chicago. His paper had a circulation many hundreds of times that of our town's entire population. Our view of reporters was mixed. We hoped for their positive opinion, knowing we'd likely never again garner such attention, but we didn't trust them. Outsiders. We answered their inquiries cautiously when we were approached in the saloon or on the street.

We took our seats and quietly awaited the arrival of the principals. Proceedings started on time. This punctuality gave us further confidence in the process.

Two well-groomed, well-dressed gentlemen stepped onto the small stage at the front of the auditorium: the opposing attorneys. We needed no announcement to quit talking at their appearance. Some among us had to resist an instinct to applaud. We were used to watching Christmas and Easter plays on this stage, so it took us a few moments to grasp that this was no make-believe production, but real life. In other circumstances, we might have dismissed them as mere city slickers or carpetbaggers. But that morning, they seemed professional and capable, and we were glad to have them in our midst. Doubtless someone would stand them drinks in the saloon after the hearing, if train schedules allowed.

The state's attorney, who would present evidence against the girl, was tall and wiry, with an extraordinarily thick head of hair. Dorothy's state-appointed defense attorney was short, bald, and rotund. A quip about the two lawyers made its way in whispers around the room: if you averaged the two men, factoring in the shapes of their bodies and amount of hair on their heads, you'd arrive at one regular human being. There were a few chuckles among us, even in such a solemn setting. But we did not lack respect for either of the men. They were officers of the court.

Whispered questions: "Where's the sheriff? Where's the girl?"

Neither was in the hall. Rather, they were waiting in the otherwise empty church. It had been agreed by all parties that the Gale girl would join the proceedings only if requested by the judge or one of the attorneys. This was not a trial, so the girl's presence was not mandatory. It was thought humane—and prudent—to spare her as much legal argument as possible, despite her vile transgressions. Such cautions for an eleven-year-old seemed reasonable. After all, this hearing was not about revenge—*"Vengeance is mine sayeth the Lord."* But we knew the girl was nearby, and we hoped to see her before the hearing was over. Not just to satisfy our curiosity, but for the sake of fairness—and to hear her side of the story.

"Please stand for the Honorable Judge Robert Barnhardt Jr.," Deputy Cutter announced from the side of the stage.

We rose as one from our folding chairs.

The Honorable Robert Barnhardt Jr.—a distinguished-looking, powerfully built man wearing a black judicial robe—entered.

The attorneys descended a few steps and assumed seats at two tables that had been placed in front of the first row. The tables faced the stage, upon which Judge Robert Barnhardt Jr. was seated in a richly upholstered wingback chair. A writing desk balanced on his lap, and a tower of law books rested on the floor at his side. From there, he could overlook the court officials and the rest of us. The arrangement was modeled on a real court room. Judge Barnhardt's piercing blue eyes gleamed cheerfully, even as he laid out the preliminary accusations against eleven-year-old Dorothy Gale.

Then the arguments.

The state went first. As this was a public hearing, there was no jury, and there would be no verdict. Judge Barnhardt would recommend either a dismissal of charges or schedule a date for a juried trial to be held in Lawrence; or he might suggest a third course of action amenable to both the prosecution and the defense. We didn't yet know *all* the details of Sheriff Hutchins's investigation, so we couldn't guess how it would come out. To say we took it all in with the greatest attention would be an understatement.

The tall, wiry prosecutor began by revealing that Sheriff Hutchins had discovered nothing illegal or unusual in Alvina Clough's financial dealings. This came as a mild surprise to us, as we'd always associated her with extreme avariciousness. Yes, she had used foreclosure laws to her advantage, incurring the predictable anger of more than a few farm families and property owners. Yet upon examination there was nothing about her business practices more predatory than those of the local bank or any other respectable financial institution. On these grounds, the prosecutor dismissed the motive of financial revenge from what he called the *murderer's profile*. This seemed a hurried and half-considered dismissal. After all, mightn't an aggrieved party be moved to murder a creditor even if a foreclosure was under-taken according to legal practices? But we didn't ponder the question for long, as we came to fully understand the prosecutor's logic when he revealed the second element of the sheriff's financial inquiry: the last will and testament of Miss Clough.

The sole beneficiary was Dorothy Gale.

The room gasped at the news, breaking into exclamations that ceased only when Judge Barnhardt hammered his gavel repeatedly on his writing desk.

"I will have order in my courtroom," he declaimed.

Though this wasn't technically a courtroom, we understood his message.

Alvina's will offered no explanation for her choice of heir.

We had no idea the old woman even knew Dorothy Gale. We'd never seen the two together, never seen Alvina in the presence of *any* child. A few of us recalled that Henry and Emily had made Alvina's acquaintance years before. They had desperately needed a loan to rebuild their windmill after it was destroyed in a storm. They repaid Alvina's loan in full, on time. No complications. While the Gales weren't present at the hearing, the prosecutor reported that the sheriff had interviewed the couple, and they had no clue why Alvina would have chosen their niece as her heir. We didn't understand Alvina's motives—but we didn't have to in order to grasp the obvious implications of the inheritance. Doesn't it make sense to suspect whoever benefits most from a crime? Isn't that the sort of thing the famous Sherlock Holmes of England would consider? Mightn't *this* speak to Dorothy's motive?

Attributing dark intent to an eleven-year-old struck us as half mad. But clearly there was much madness surrounding the killing.

"Where does the girl claim to have been during those days and nights she was missing?" Judge Barnhardt asked.

"A phantasmagorical land of witches and wizards," the prosecutor answered.

We'd already heard tell of the girl's far-fetched yarn. To hear it now stated aloud in an official setting raised another outburst of exclamations and scandalized commentary, sending the judge back to his gavel.

Bang, bang, bang!

"Dorothy Gale maintains that she's innocent of this crime," the tall attorney continued, "because when the murder occurred, she was far away in a land populated by inanimate objects and talking animals. For example, a lion and a scarecrow, that were as lucid and *possessed of divine souls* as human beings. Consider the heresy of that statement. *That's* her alibi? A land characterized by the darkest kind of magic. A godless, downright infernal place. The story is unbelievable and completely useless as an alibi. However, it tells us much about this eleven-year-old girl accused of committing a crime that none of us would have thought possible for one of such tender years. Rather than being shame-faced, the Gale girl seems almost proud of her wicked delusion. From the first time she described this blasphemous paradise to poor Mrs. Pendleton, the girl has made no attempt to depict her story as anything but real. She is young—true. But not so young that the basic distinction between good and evil is beyond her reach. We do not raise our children in ignorance of the Lord's word. Along with the rest of this fine community's children, she regularly attended your Reverend Richter's Sunday school. So what's the Gale girl's excuse? There can be no excuse."

This was a very good attorney. He'd have made a fine preacher, though we all agreed he was just as surely doing the Lord's work here in Sunbonnet's church hall. The Lord loves justice too.

"But that's not the worst of the girl's story, Your Honor," the lawyer continued. "I've spoken of blasphemy, paganism, and sacrilege. And yet, hard as it may be to believe, there is worse. Dorothy Gale has repeated this most shameful part of her yarn more than once and to more than one witness. She says that while transported to this pagan landscape, a period that coincides with this heinous murder in Sunbonnet, she 'killed a witch.' Those are her words, ladies and gentlemen. In her very own words, Dorothy Gale committed murder."

We'd heard rumor of the Gale girl's confession, but the power of hearing it spoken in public cannot be overstated. The audience gasped, and more than one of the townswomen paled before our eyes and fainted in their chairs. There was a ruckus and rambling of movement and concerned voices as the judge once again slammed his gavel to restore order.

Bang, bang, bang!

The afflicted women were quickly carried from the auditorium. Ladies of a similarly sensitive nature were advised to leave with them. Most stayed.

The lawyer picked up where he'd left off, the details growing only more gruesome:

"The Gale girl confessed to tossing a bucket full of liquid onto the 'witch,' causing the victim to *melt*. The parallels to the Alvina Clough murder are obvious. I will not belabor them except to emphasize two points. First, poor Miss Clough was indeed 'melted' by a brutal inundation of lye, a chemical known to scientists as potassium hydroxide. Used for domestic purposes such as soap making, lye is readily available at any general store or in the storage sheds of most farms. However, don't be fooled by its easy acquisition. It can be a deadly weapon. There's the obvious and immediate damage to skin and soft tissue, which in itself is enough to cause death by shock. And the chemical is even more deadly if ingested or inhaled, actions likely to occur if a victim is unexpectedly 'splashed' in the face.

Residue of lye was discovered in a bucket discarded in a corner of Miss Clough's kitchen. Can you imagine a more gruesome or painful death?"

He turned from the judge to us. "My apologies, folks, for my unpleasant words. The law requires that I must follow where the facts take me."

Many of us nodded our assent, even if we were half sickened.

"What's the second point you wanted to make, Counselor?" Judge Barnhardt asked.

"It has to do with the second crucial word contained in the Gale girl's confession. 'Witch.' I approach this topic as respectfully as possible. I take no pleasure in defaming either this good community or the memory of Miss Alvina Clough. However, I'd be remiss if I failed to point out that for many decades Miss Clough was regarded in a less than charitable light by some of the townsfolk of Sunbonnet. Generations of children referred to her as a . . ." He stopped, obviously pained by the word. "Again, my apologies, good people of Sunbonnet. But in the interest of justice, I must say the word aloud—a *witch*. Yes, this proud but reclusive woman who came to such a brutal end was known to generations of children as a witch. It can come as no surprise that Dorothy Gale also thought of her by that term. Her stated 'recollection' indicates exactly that."

We sat silently in our seats. Though this made none of us proud, we understood the necessity of his honesty.

"I know that name-calling among children goes against the Christian values of this community, and I hold the town blameless. After all, children *can* be cruel. But in regards to the details of *this* case, the connection is obvious. Thus, the girl's 'confession' about her actions in her 'other' world reveals precisely what happened here."

"And for clarity's sake," the judge said, "what is it that happened, Counselor?"

"Dorothy Gale murdered poor Alvina Clough."

As we had already come to the same conclusion, we did not react with the kind of exclamations or whispered commentary that had accompanied some of the prosecutor's previous remarks. We nodded among ourselves, sometimes sighing that such a thing was possible. What kind of world was this?

Then the ever-astute Judge Barnhardt put a most insightful question to the prosecutor.

"If Dorothy Gale is guilty of committing the crime," the judge began—we all admired the legal propriety of using the word *if*—"then what might have possessed her to incorporate such a thinly veiled admission of said crime into her sincerely held and quite original delusion?"

"An excellent question, Your Honor," the prosecutor said. "Why would a girl capable of such defilement confess to her crime without prompting? I believe I have an answer. Before I offer it, allow me to answer the final part of your question. You suggest that the Oz fantasy is an actual delusion, a psychological occurrence, thereby implying the girl is powerless to do anything but be swept up in it. May I offer an alternative?"

"Go on, Counselor."

"I suggest the girl only pretends to believe her blasphemous yarn. It is no mere delusion resulting from a bump on the head or a reaction to the fearsomeness of a tornado. Rather, I suggest she invented it as a cover for her crimes. That she has chosen to include diabolical elements—witches and wizards and magic of all sorts—indicates her wish to be thought guilty of a blasphemous brand of insanity, but not murder. I base these assertions on testimony offered by Sunbonnet's highly trusted physician,

Edmund Ward. Dr. Ward noted that, while in his personal office, where only hours before the girl had first given name to her magical land of Oz, he noticed that his file cabinet—"

The defense attorney rose. "I object, Your Honor. Didn't we stipulate that the matter of the doctor's file cabinet would not be introduced at this hearing? Didn't we agree not to question my client's intent as regards to the origin of her claims?"

"We did," Judge Barnhardt said. He turned to the prosecutor. "You will leave discussion of the file cabinet for another time, Counselor. If at all."

"Yes, sir."

Until now, it had not occurred to us that the three men had already met to discuss the proceedings. But of course, such a meeting would have occurred. Smoothing the path of justice is the role of professionals.

"Please return to the question I posed, Counselor," the judge said to the prosecutor. "Why would the Gale girl have mentioned the 'melting of a witch' if doing so serves as a kind of confession to an actual crime?"

"One theory put forth by Dr. Ward," the prosecutor said, "is that the girl's seeming confession may be a cold-blooded form of boasting."

Again the room erupted.

The gavel came down half a dozen times or more.

Order was restored.

The rotund defense attorney stood again. "Your Honor, as stated before, we agreed not to address my client's intent as regards her story until this case proceeds to trial, *if* it proceeds to trial."

Judge Barnhardt nodded. "Yes, Counselor. We will drop this line of questioning immediately."

"Allow me to address one more question, Your Honor."
The prosecutor cleared his throat and faced us. His features,
which had borne a serious expression from the start, grew even
more dour. "I look out over this crowd of God-fearing citizens
and I know you are asking yourselves, *'How can such a thing as a
child who is a killer be possible?'* It's natural for any Christian man
or woman to be deeply troubled by such a question. For a spiritual answer, I leave that to your good reverend; I trust he will
soothe your anguished souls. My responsibility is to provide
you with the facts. Children *do* kill, with premeditation and
utmost cruelty. It's not common but neither is it unknown. For
the sake of brevity, allow me to remind you of just one of many
instances. No doubt you read about it a few years back. The
case shocked the nation. The evidence was unequivocal. An
infamous young man named Jesse Pomeroy committed a pair
of cold-blooded murders at the tender age of fourteen. Today
Pomeroy is serving a life sentence in the Massachusetts State
Prison. Tragically, his victims were also children: a girl of ten
and a boy of four. Sad to say, such things do happen. We live in
a fallen world among fallen people of *all* ages. But all is not lost.
Our faith in God and our American justice system will see us
through. It has before; it always will."

"Any further comments?" the judge said.

"What more could there be?" the prosecutor said.

The judge glowered. "I do not appreciate arrogance in my
courtroom, Counselor."

No one dared point out to Judge Barnhardt that this was
not technically a courtroom.

"My apologies, Your Honor."

The judge turned to the defense attorney. "Have you rebut-
tals, Counselor?"

"Not at this time," the round man said.

The judge sat back, fingers drumming on an arm of his chair. For a moment, we thought the proceeding might be over. It was not.

"I'd like to ask the Gale girl a few questions," the judge said, "if that's acceptable to defense counsel. Seeing as this is a hearing and not a trial . . ."

"I have no objection," said the girl's attorney.

★   ★   ★

The church hall was thick with anticipation by the time the sheriff entered with Dorothy.

It may sound foolish now, but we wondered if her crime had left some blemish upon her face or some crook to her posture or some hesitation in her step. It had not. She looked the same. Actually, she looked healthier than we remembered; she'd benefitted from the attention of the reverend and his wife, who'd kept her safe, warm, and well-fed. The reverend had spent many hours every day talking to her about the consolations of the Lord. She'd heard such things before in church services and Sunday school, but we had no doubt the effect was more powerful when the reverend imparted the Good News directly. Although the girl had asked to see her aunt and uncle during her three weeks with the Richters, Henry and Emily did not visit. Henry spent most of his time wandering aimlessly about the refuse that had been the Gale property. Having discharged his three farmhands shortly after the twister, he'd accomplished nothing. He hadn't cleared the wreckage, rebuilt the house or windmill, mended fences, or re-tilled the churned-up fields.

The only time we saw him around town was when he was drinking in the saloon, which he'd taken to doing more frequently since the twister. Being a silent and sullen drunk, he might as well not have been there at all. No one paid him any mind. Not even when he began carrying around his Remington .44 revolver, issued during the War Between the States. We took no alarm. The only person he'd likely shoot was himself. And for this we'd hardly blame him. A week or so after the twister, Emily was stricken with a seizure that left her partly crippled, so she spent her time in the borrowed bed in their makeshift home in the barn. Perhaps we should have known that more ill would arise from the Gale place, even with Dorothy elsewhere, but we were understandably preoccupied by other matters.

The sheriff led Dorothy to a seat beside her attorney.

A tear rolled down the girl's face, and she whispered, "I never killed anything, willingly. Never, never . . ."

Her attorney glanced nervously about the hall and then patted his young client's shoulder. "Collect yourself," he said. "Pull yourself together, girl."

"I would like to ask the girl a question," the judge said. "May I, Counselor?"

Her attorney moved behind Dorothy and lightly grasped the girl's shoulders and straightened her posture. "Now, Your Honor, you may ask my client your question."

"Thank you, Counselor." The judge shifted his attention to Dorothy. "Young lady, have you ever heard the biblical quote from Exodus *'Thou shall not suffer a witch to live'*?"

Dorothy said nothing. Perhaps she was stunned by the great man's attentions.

"You may shake your head yes or no," Judge Barnhardt continued, softening his tone.

The girl mumbled something we couldn't hear.

"Can you please speak up, missy?"

"Those words sound familiar." Her reedy voice was barely audible.

"Do you understand the quote?"

She shook her head no.

"It means a good person should not allow a witch to live." The judge leaned forward. "Do you remember hearing those words? In church perhaps? Or Sunday school?"

"Maybe."

"Is that why you killed 'the witch'?" the judge asked. "Did you do it because the Bible tells you to do it? To be good?"

She did not move.

The hall was silent.

"Is that why you did it?" the judge pressed.

She shook her head again.

"Do you believe the Bible is *wrong* on this account?"

She remained quiet.

"Didn't you tell Dr. Ward and your aunt and uncle that you'd killed a witch in this 'other' place you were transported to?"

"That's what I told them."

"Were you lying, Dorothy?"

"No, sir."

"Then did you kill a witch or didn't you?"

"I didn't *mean* to kill her," Dorothy said.

We sat up straighter in our chairs.

"But why not, since the Bible says it's right?" Cleverly, the judge spoke to her like she was an ally. "And it's not just in Exodus. If memory serves, it also says in Leviticus that a witch or wizard shall surely be put to death. It's written right there. So perhaps that's why you did it?"

"I'd never do that."

"Never? How can you be so sure?"

"Because not all witches are bad."

A gasp from the entire room.

Dorothy seemed only then to notice all her neighbors packed into the room. She dropped her head on the desk, dissolving in tears.

Judge Barnhardt, who hadn't a cruel bone in his body, addressed a sobbing Dorothy. "Just tell us what happened, young lady. You can make all this simple. You'll feel better. Tell us what happened with Miss Clough and why."

The girl didn't—or couldn't—speak.

Reverend Richter strode forward. "The girl's had enough, Your Honor. We might leave off questioning her at this time. You have all you need from this hearing."

Judge Barnhardt didn't seem offended by the reverend's interruption. "I believe you're right, Reverend. This hearing stands adjourned." And with that, the judge brought the gavel down on the lap desk one last time.

By the time the 9:33 train left the station that night, carrying the visiting legal professionals, we'd learned this: the day's hearing would be the first and last of the proceedings.

The judge and the two attorneys settled the details in a private meeting after the hearing. They arrived at the most fitting solution for the Gale girl—a decision at once compassionate to the wicked child, respectful of our community's safety, responsible to justice, and considerate of the memory of our fallen neighbor, Alvina Clough.

CHAPTER 8

Once again, I was made to wait in the women's recreation room while the nurse brought Dorothy from her bedroom to the dining hall. I don't understand the impractical protocol of my being directed to wait in there rather than in the public lobby, the superintendent's office, on a bench in the parklike grounds, or even in the empty dining hall itself. Do they think I'll be put off my inquiry by being briefly enclosed with the patients in this space? Don't they know I am a professional, even if I'm a woman? It's disheartening how many in this supposedly forward-thinking field consider that designation, *professional woman*, to be an oxymoron. It is like the term *lady doctor*. No matter. Being forced to wait among patients isn't worthy of a confrontation, particularly as I likely will have more important matters to address with them soon enough. Matters of Dorothy G.'s well-being.

A different set of women populated the recreation room this time, though they exhibited many of the same behaviors as their counterparts. One woman in particular stood out. She had a nest of gray hair piled carelessly atop her head and was huddled in one corner, clutching a yellowed quarter page torn from an old newspaper. She read aloud from the scrap.

Or, should I say, pretended to read. I have no idea what was actually printed on the scrap, but the "news" she shared with the women gathered around her was an imaginative blend of history and romance that would have made for good premises in the popular press. Words and images fell beautifully from her lips, and her appreciative audience was uncharacteristically quiet and well-behaved. One story bled into the next. It was all ephemeral, like so many dreams, even though she presented the tales as being straight from the newspaper. I lack the literary skills to reproduce her narratives here. However, I can't help but reflect on what a delight it would be to one day pick up a periodical on a city street and discover written there accounts not of crime and corruption, but stories like hers.

★ ★ ★

When the head nurse arrived to show me to the dining hall, the woman with the nest of gray hair was still "reading" from her scrap. I'd like to have talked to her. Later, when I asked after her, none of the staff knew who or what I was talking about. It was almost as if I myself had conjured the woman in the recreation room.

"Why just those? Why don't you lay all the cards on the table, Dr. Evelyn Grace Wilford?"

"These twenty-two cards have the most vivid pictures in the deck. The most important ones. So we don't have to use all the cards. After all, we're not playing any kind of game."

"We're only interested in the pictures?"

"Yes. Do you find them interesting, Dorothy?"

"They're pretty. But old-fashioned."

"That's because they're old."

"Why are we talking about *these* pictures? What makes them special?"

"For centuries people have looked at these pictures and drawn meaning from them."

"Meaning? What kind of meaning? I told you I won't have anything to do with fortune-telling."

"This is nothing like that. What I meant to say was that the pictures on these cards have stood for strikingly similar things to people from different places and even different centuries. It's my professional opinion that they contain a kind of coded, pictorial language that speaks to an important human commonality."

"What are you talking about?"

"Let me put it another way: some people, like the soothsayer who was run out of Sunbonnet, make claims that these cards can reveal the future. I don't believe such claims for a moment."

"Because you're a scientist?"

"Because I have common sense."

"Then what's special about them?"

"Just because these cards can't tell the future doesn't mean they can't help us understand things about the present. Or the past."

"How?"

"I can't say exactly. All I know is that these images have been important to so many for so long that they *must* contain some universal truths that speak to us."

"The cards speak?"

"They don't talk, if that's what you're asking. But I believe they communicate without words to the secret parts of our minds."

"The parts of our minds where we keep secrets?"

"No—the parts of our minds that keep secrets from us."

"That makes no sense. My mind may keep secrets from others, but it doesn't keep secrets from *me*. I know what I know."

"Are you sure?"

". . ."

"But if your mind *did* keep some things secret, then you wouldn't know."

" What do you call this part of the mind that keeps secrets from itself?"

"I don't have a name for it."

"How's it work?"

"I don't know, Dorothy."

"Then what makes you think it's real?"

"It makes sense to me."

"That's not a very scientific answer."

"True. But haven't you ever experienced something that you know is real even if you can't explain how such a thing can possibly be?"

"Of course I have. You know that."

"Oz."

". . . Yes."

"Some things just *are*. We don't have to understand them to gain something important from them. Like these cards. You don't mind talking about a few colorful pictures, do you?"

"It's better than sitting in those rocking chairs they make us sit in all day. This is your own idea? Or your professor's?"

"My own."

"Am I some kind of experiment?"

"Professor James likes to say that everything in life is an experiment. But no, you're more than just an experiment to me."

"What am I then?"

"A very bright girl who'd like to help me with an experiment."

"All right, Dr. Evelyn Grace Wilford."

"I'm going to ask you to pick a card. But not at random. Remember, this is no game of chance."

"So how do I pick?"

"Pick the one that reminds you most of you."

"Me?"

"Yes."

". . ."

". . ."

"This one."

"The Fool. Why'd you pick this?"

"He has a little dog. See? That's Toto. My sweet dog. I wouldn't want to be a picture on any card without Toto on it too."

"Any other reasons you chose it, Dorothy?"

"Look at the other cards. I'm not an Empress or an Emperor or Pope or the Sun."

"How does it make you feel to be the Fool?"

"I feel like one. I went from the farm to Oz and back, only to end up here . . . What else am I but a fool?"

"Some people consider the Fool to be the most powerful
of all the major arcana."

"The major what?"

"These picture cards are called arcana."

"How is a fool powerful?"

"The Fool is best suited to move freely between worlds
. . . like you, Dorothy. I'm glad you chose that card. I
think it's a very good sign."

"Are you telling my fortune?"

"I was just commenting, which I shouldn't do. You can set
that card back in its place. Now, pick one that makes
you think of the Wizard in Oz."

"That's easy. This one. The Magician."

"Why?"

"He has a lot of power throughout the lands. But it was all
gained through trickery. Still, it was power. And he did
accomplish things that were amazing, even if they were
only magic tricks. He was very likeable too. A show-
man. He'd have sold out theaters in Boston and New
York, pulling rabbits out of his hat, if his balloon had
landed him there instead of the Emerald City."

"The hot air balloon he used to leave Oz?"

"I keep forgetting I told you about these things."

"Not everything. Just what I read in your file."

"Will you put the notes you're taking today into my file?"

"No. These notes are private. Just for you and me . . .
Which card reminds you of Glinda?"

"This one."

"The Chariot? Why did you choose that?"

"Because Glinda can come and go as she pleases. Fast as
a chariot. Faster. She's very beautiful and wise, but her

ability to be here one moment and somewhere else the next is the most astonishing thing about her. She taught me how to transport myself magically too."

"By knocking the heels of the magical shoes together?"

"Yes."

"Which card reminds you of the Wicked Witch?"

"What if there's more than one?"

"Pick as many cards as you please."

". . . These three."

"Death, the Devil, the Tower of Destruction."

"You don't have to ask why I picked them. Just look at the pictures."

"Let's try something a little different. I'll show you a card, and you tell me who it reminds you of. Don't think about it—just give me the first name that pops into your head."

"Okay."

". . ."

"That card makes me think of the Scarecrow."

"Why does the Hanged Man remind you of the Scarecrow?

"Look at him hanging there upside down—so strange. But otherwise he could be a scarecrow. And look at his face. He doesn't seem much bothered by his troubles. That's how the Scarecrow seemed when I first met him, hanging up on his pole."

"And this card?"

"That one reminds me of Uncle Henry."

"I was thinking we'd just talk about Oz . . ."

"Oh, sorry."

"No, please. Go ahead and name anybody who comes to mind. Why does the Hermit remind you of your Uncle Henry?"

"Because even though Uncle Henry is with us on the farm every day, he's never *really* with us. He's alone in his own world. Always. And he hates my aunt and me for intruding on his life. He hates everyone for the same reason. He's sour. That's why he's the Hermit."

"And this card?"

"Judgment? That's the whole town of Sunbonnet. See the people at the bottom of the card? They're the towns-folk. They're all naked. They'd sure hate that! And the angel blowing the horn from up above? That's Rever-end Richter. He's no angel in real life, even if he thinks he is."

"And this one?"

"The moon? It reminds me of Alvina Clough."

"Alvina?"

"See the dogs barking at her? That's how everyone always acted. Always barking at her. And the lobster rising out of the waters to snap his claws at her. That was the town too. Snap, snap. They hated her just because she kept herself to herself, like the moon. But sometimes she let a sliver of herself show. Even when you couldn't see her, you knew she was there. Until she wasn't."

"Did you know her, Dorothy? Did you ever talk to her?"

"No, but I knew *of* her. We'd see her sometimes in town. And some of us children were cruel to her. But I wasn't."

"Why not?"

"Because I'm not a cruel person. That's a silly question, Dr. Evelyn Grace Wilford."

"It was."

"I'm glad we're agreed on that."

"But what about these three cards? Death, the Devil, and the Tower of Destruction?"

"I already used them for the Wicked Witch."

"You can use cards more than once."

"I don't need to use them more than once. Those three cards remind me of the Wicked Witch. That's all."

"And this one reminds you of Alvina?"

"Yes."

"So they're really two different people, aren't they, Dorothy? The witch and Alvina."

"Yes. Just like I always said. Give me another card. This is fun."

"What about Justice? Sword in one hand, scale in the other."

"You know who this one reminds me of?"

"Tell me."

"You guess. Just this once."

"Judge Barnhardt?"

"Who?"

"The judge from your hearing."

"Not even close."

"Then who does it remind you of?"

"You, Dr. Evelyn Grace Wilford."

CHAPTER 9

There could be no timelier message for us than John 1:9, which Reverend Richter quoted from the pulpit at Sunday service a few days after the Gale girl's hearing: *"If we confess our sins, He is faithful and just to forgive us our sins, and to cleanse us from all unrighteousness."* Hearing these words, we townsfolk exchanged reassuring glances in the pews. It had been a trying few weeks. We were more in need of a reminder of the Lord's goodness than we'd realized when first we took our seats that morning in our well-tended white clapboard church. The reverend knew us well. Maybe better than we knew ourselves. *"Cleanse us from all unrighteousness . . ."* Proximity to sinfulness had sullied us. Yes, we had gossiped. Yes, we had gorged our fascination with the grotesqueries of recent events. Yes, we had suffered pride when we compared our lives to those of Dorothy Gale and her wretched aunt and uncle. So we let the Lord's words wash over us. *"Cleanse us from all unrighteousness . . ."* It was good. But we did not miss the requirement that John 1:9 specifies for the acquisition of divine forgiveness—that we confess our sins.

Simple enough.

Yet even on this Sunday, as the Gale girl spent her final hours in our good reverend's home before being sent away to

Topeka's state institution for what promised to be many years of confinement, she still refused to confess to any sin whatsoever. Not to indulging as imaginary cohorts a wizard and a quartet of witches—stand-ins for the ungodly impulses of her own soul. Not to creating a painfully public spectacle from her patently absurd alibi—a yarn pagan enough to set any good Christian's teeth on edge. Not to murdering Alvina Clough. No apologies. No acceptance of responsibility. Only extenuation: "But Oz is real!" And denial: "I didn't kill Alvina!"

We knew the reverend to be a devout and determined man, yet even his private exhortations, delivered day after day from a chair beside the girl's bed in his upstairs guest room, had failed to move her. Joshua 7:19: *"Give, I pray thee, glory to the Lord God of Israel, and make confession unto him; and tell me now what thou hast done; hide it not from me."* When pressed to name any regret, the Gale girl claimed only to be sorry she'd come home to Kansas. Of all things! Ingratitude is also a sin. The girl had much to be grateful for. Consider how Reverend Richter's choice of John 1:9 as his Bible citation that Sunday illustrated the generous attitude he held out to her, the hope of forgiveness. He might as easily have chosen Mark 3:29. *"He that shall blaspheme against the Holy Ghost hath never forgiveness . . ."* But that was not the reverend's message. Nor was it ours. Oh, we readily acknowledged our own sinfulness these past weeks when it came to engaging in gossip and perverse fascination and pride, but we remained unrepentant on one point. We had never demonstrated an unwillingness to forgive, if only the girl had also been willing to confess her transgressions. What greater openness might we have shown to her, particularly considering the diabolical nature of her offenses? Dorothy Gale was indeed most fortunate.

The conclusive example of moral generosity offered the girl during this period was the legal agreement worked out immediately after her hearing by Judge Barnhardt and the two attorneys with whom he traveled his circuit. These men had undertaken a judicial task that might have tested Solomon. The crime was heinous, but the Gale girl was only eleven years old and had never before demonstrated a predisposition for violence or deceit. What was the court to do to a child charged with a capital offense? Solomonic indeed. We learned that the state of Illinois had recently created a separate court for cases involving legal minors, a first in our great nation. But as Kansas had no like process, the judge and his team were faced with only hard choices. Judge Barnhardt was up to the task. With the assistance of Reverend Richter, Sheriff Hutchins, Mayor Watt-Smith, Carson Whitfield, and Dr. Ward, the good judge arrived at a decision worthy of . . . well, Solomon. The Gale girl was more fortunate than she ever admitted.

In lieu of a murder trial and certain conviction, the girl would be committed for a period of not less than seven years to the state insane asylum. Commitment papers would allude to her reckless disappearance at the time of the tornado; her subsequent story of Oz, the wretched and impious elements of which were undeniable proof that she was a present danger to society—this at a time when her poor aunt needed her ministrations; and most significantly, her responsibility for the brutal death of poor Alvina Clough. Technically, the girl was adjudged by reason of insanity to be innocent of murder. That she willfully upheld her preposterous claims against all assaults worked in her favor as her stubbornness evidenced an unreasoned response. Who but a madman, or mad girl, would hold so determinedly to an absurd and repugnant tale? Simply put, the girl had fallen into the deep dark well of insanity, perhaps in the terrifying first moments of the twister, perhaps in utero. The how, why, and when didn't matter to us. All that mattered was that she was mad.

The state of Kansas had a place for such poor souls. We were kind enough to put her there.

★ ★ ★

After that Sunday service, most of us found reason to linger in town longer than usual. There was the regular socializing in the church hall, where earlier in the week we'd witnessed the girl's public hearing. The rows of chairs had been removed and stored, and the big room was returned from magisterial formality to comfortable commonality. We mingled there, unhurried, complimenting the reverend's sermon and drinking cups of coffee or tea as we passed from card table to card table, sampling the finest homemade baked goods this side of the Missouri River. Twenty-five cents for a freshly baked cherry pie . . . all in the service of the Annual Church Fund. Reverend Richter liked to joke: "If only all good works could be so delicious!" The forty-five minutes or so that we usually spent in such circumstances lasted well over an hour and a half this Sunday. This had something to do with the withering intensity of the previous weeks and our need to return to normality. We talked about farming, housekeeping, machinery, cooking, politics, children, livestock, sewing, in any of a hundred reassuringly ordinary practicalities. The unspoken element of all these conversations, however, was anything but ordinary: our neighbor Alvina had been murdered. The Gale girl was to be exiled this very day to the state asylum in Topeka. Henry and Emily Gale were disgraced for the un-Christian manner in which

they had brought up their charge. *And yet*, despite these occurrences, we townsfolk were free now to return to the simple,
God-fearing lives we'd enjoyed before the fateful twister initiated the havoc. With reassurance drawn from every ordinary
comment or observation shared between bites of cherry pie,
was it any wonder we lingered so long in the church hall? Some
might have stayed the rest of the afternoon. But, as the Bible
says, all things have their time and so we could not stay much
past 12:30, even though Dorothy Gale was not scheduled to
board her train until 3:37. We were, almost all of us, quietly
determined to remain in town to witness her departure.

After we'd socialized in the church hall, some of us drifted
to the Sunbonnet Grill to enjoy an uncharacteristically long
lunch. Others moved their little parties to the park, where con-
struction of the new gazebo was nearly complete. Still others
visited friends who lived near the station, ensuring themselves
good places from which to witness the Gale girl's last
moments in Sunbonnet. Naturally she remained on our minds,
even as we resisted mentioning her name aloud. To do so was
to acknowledge a fascination with her monstrous crime that
crossed from responsible civic interest to perverse curiosity.
Nothing like this had ever happened in Sunbonnet, nor in any
other town we'd heard of. Doubtless, we were fallen creatures,
as are we all, so how could we not desire both normality *and* to
see the whole sordid affair to its end? How could we be anywhere but the train station to watch the 3:37 pull out with the
murderous child aboard? So we loitered and lollygagged in
town that afternoon, and by three-thirty a crowd of us had
gathered on the platform at the station.

Meantime, the reverend and Mrs. Richter had returned to
their house after the last parishioner left the cherry pie–scented

church hall. Once there, the good couple unlocked the girl's second-floor bedroom and helped her to pack a small valise of her possessions. The final few articles were delivered in the dead of night by Henry. It was a hot day, but Mrs. Richter dressed the Gale girl in her winter coat and hat since she'd need these things in the years to come at the state institution. Sheriff Hutchins and Dr. Ward met the Richters and the girl on the porch, and soon the five of them crossed the neatly tended front garden and climbed into the fine surrey that belonged to Carson Whitfield, the cattle buyer and grain elevator administrator. They made their way from the house to the station. Some older children ran alongside the surrey, shouting things at the Gale girl, until the sheriff stopped the wagon dead in its tracks and chased off the unruly youths.

Those of us waiting on the platform grew quiet when the surrey approached.

The train pulled in a few minutes early and sat hissing like a breathless beast.

The girl climbed down, moving with her small party through the station, and emerged on the platform. Her movements and expression betrayed nothing. No fear, no regret, no shame . . . If anything, she seemed excited to board the train, which might be expected of an eleven-year-old who had never ventured more than a few miles out of town—discounting her ridiculous claim of distant transport via tornado. A few of the younger children in the crowd called out, "Goodbye, Dorothy!" Their intent was innocent enough, but in each case their parents quite rightfully yanked them close and insisted on silence. This strange girl was not their friend and never had been. Dorothy boarded the train without glancing back, almost as if she hadn't seen us, though we numbered in the hundreds.

Is it possible she didn't see us? Just how broken had her mind become? And if she didn't see us, what diabolical things did she see instead? Witches, talking beasts, flying monkeys? None of us could begin to imagine, and even if we could, we knew better than to tempt it. She had ignored even the low grumblings of the bitterest among us, "child of Satan," "murderess," "beast." Most townsfolk didn't approve of the epithets.

Yet we couldn't help but wonder if Dorothy's acceptance of the characterizations indicated a begrudging acknowledgment of the truth. In any case, she climbed aboard the train and disappeared inside with the sheriff, who carried her small bag and would see her all the way to Topeka and the waiting asylum attendants.

Others boarded the train too: a half dozen out-of-town newspaper reporters.

We were relieved to see them go. They'd arrived in the days preceding the hearing, a ragged and noisy bunch dressed in loud suits and boater hats. Jokers all. Drinkers. At the Peabody Hotel or the Sunbonnet Grill, their money was good, and so we bit our tongues. But we watched them cautiously.

Most everything they wrote about Alvina's murder and the Gale girl's involvement in the crime was too clever by half, as they didn't much care for obvious truth. That was boring to them, and presumably to their readers. So they found fault where there was none. The worst of the lot was a beady-eyed bastard from the newspaper in Lawrence. He was a Kansan, born and bred. So he had no excuse. Guile and unbridled ambition know no state boundaries, and he succumbed to the filthy lucre of yellow journalism. He called the Gale girl's hearing a "witch trial" and tried to turn the girl's own unholy associations against the proceedings by casually linking the good work of Judge Barnhardt to a misbegotten historical incident among a radical Puritanical sect two centuries before! All for the sake of rhetorical cleverness, a journalistic flourish, a pun. Such misshaping of the truth should not be allowed in a democracy. Yes, the reporter was careful enough in the body of his story to shape the facts into a semblance of accuracy, but the objectionable and weighted term *witch trial* implied a lack of judicial integrity. Bah! The legal proceeding wasn't a trial in the first place—it was a hearing. Absent a verdict, how could there have been any miscarriage of justice? The opposing attorneys had agreed on a humanitarian course of action, overseen by the judge and our town's most distinguished gentlemen.

All of this cynical newswriting amounted to very little. However, the reporters did not leave Sunbonnet without causing damage, as one of them posted a personal letter that would prove disruptive indeed.

CHAPTER 10

I arrived for my final visit with Dorothy G.

I'd tucked my train ticket for Sunbonnet into my hand-bag and left my baggage in the hired carriage awaiting me at the asylum gates. But this visit did not go as before. I was told by the supervising physician that Dorothy was unavailable for interview or observation and would remain so for the rest of the day. At first, the doctor and other staff resisted my efforts to discern why this was. They assured me she was in good physical health and that I needn't worry. I was not assured. After I called to bear whatever professional weight I could muster from my association with Professor James, I learned that Dorothy was being treated with chloral hydrate. This is commonly used to slow the heart rate and make the subject calm or, depending on the dosage, nearly comatose. Further, I learned that she was injected "regularly" with the sedative. None of this was noted in her file. When I objected to the treatment, the supervising physician told me that use of the drug was far more humane than wrestling the patient into chains or a leather harness. But why would *any* such measures be necessary when it came to Dorothy? I demanded. In perverse answer, the physician revealed that he had surreptitiously observed all my interviews with Dorothy—what right had he to do so? He concluded I'd been grossly deceived by the girl, whose demeanor in my presence was different from what it was with the hospital staff. He spoke of her rages and tantrums, neither of which I consider natural to the gentle spirit I've come to know. Anyone subjected to the rigors of this place would grow to anger. Particularly if insanity didn't constitute a significant part of one's makeup. I'm increasingly convinced this is the case with Dorothy G. When I voiced my objections to the supervising physician, he reacted with near violence, reminding me that the eleven-year-old I described as gentle had murdered an old woman by melting off her face with lye. When I told him I doubted her guilt, this sent him into a fit of disapprobation about womankind's inability to confront hard truths. I denied him the dignity of a response. He grew silent, staring at me as if I were mad—as if he wished *I* were locked up in this facility and subject to his "care." I saw much darkness in his face. Then he stormed from the room. The encounter affirmed my decision to travel to Sunbonnet, not only to gain insights into my research subject, Dorothy G., but to determine if she is indeed a murderess who belongs here in this wretched place.

If I cannot prove she is innocent of the crime and thereby free her from the rigors of this asylum, she will be lost to sanity before this year is over. Lost forever. Even as flexible and sturdy a mind as Dorothy's will be broken. It is also true that I possess no professional mandate to undertake an investigation of a months-old murder. I possess no training to accomplish it. But I am not a fool, and so perhaps I will not be fooled, as others in Sunbonnet seem to have been. Contemplating the stakes, what choice do I have but to try?

Taking my leave, I glanced from the open carriage back to the turreted, yellow brick buildings and manicured grounds of the Topeka Insane Asylum. From a distance the place looks as tranquil as a picture postcard. As I settled into the carriage, pulling the buffalo hide onto my lap to stay warm, I recalled the gray-haired old lady I'd seen in the recreation room "reading" from a yellowed scrap of newspaper. The woman's will to imagine was admirable. Enviable even. But there's nothing enviable about her life. And then I had a terrible thought: *Fifty years from now, might Dorothy G. end up like that old woman, standing in the same corner of the recreation room, "reading" aloud from a news clipping about the goings-on in an imaginary world far more beautiful than the one she's forced to inhabit?*

PART TWO

"I never killed anything, willingly," she sobbed, "and even if I wanted to, how could I kill the Wicked Witch?"

—*The Wizard of Oz*
L. Frank Baum, 1900

CHAPTER 11

September 12, 1896

Dear Professor James,

What is a physician to do when the most serious threat to her patient's well-being is not primarily medical or psychological, but instead results from powerful, externally imposed circumstances based on a terrible miscarriage of justice? By what authority can we physicians act in ways that do not draw directly upon our training? It is true that the body and mind are the domains over which we are licensed to practice. Our charge is to heal human beings, not society. But what is our responsibility to a patient when it is society, and not a pathogen, that threatens a patient's life and future prospects? We are not trained as electricians, yet we may still switch on an electrified lamp to better illuminate a room for a patient suffering, from cataracts. To fail to do so would be unprofessional and cruel. What is the limit to which we can press such nonmedical acts of service? Traveling to a small Kansas town to investigate a murder entails more than merely flipping on an electrified light. But if it is only in that small town that an antidote may be found to cure a patient's otherwise terminal diagnosis . . . well, my good professor, what else is one to do?

I close my eyes and listen closely.

I hear your words in my head, answering a litany of questions, even at this distance of space and time: *"Methinks the lady doth protest too much."*

You and the Bard are correct. I am full of doubts about my current course of action. I worry about the ethics of engaging outside my professional training, as well as my capacity to do so successfully. All I know of crime or investigation I gained by having read *Bleak House* and Wilkie Collins and a few Sherlock Holmes stories. I know they are mere shadow plays of real crime. But then I think of your words in *The Principles of Psychology*, which have long inspired me: *"The effort of attention is thus the essential phenomenon of will."*

And so I am arrived in Sunbonnet.

Attentive.

I believe I have made some advances in the girl's case.

But first, you may be wondering what progress I made with the research project—generously funded by your institution—that brought me to Kansas in the first place.

I found Dorothy Gale to be bright and forthcoming. Her commitment to the reality of her "envisioned objects," which include good and bad witches, a wizard, talking animals, an animate scarecrow, and other outlandish beings, remains strong. Despite this bounty of material, I discovered that I was both willing and enthusiastic to abandon my experimental protocol at the first opportunity. Dorothy responded to the Tarot card pictures not with parallels to her imaginary world, but to her real one, to people actually living in Sunbonnet. For the purposes of my experiment, I ought to have guided her back to her land of Oz. I understand that an unyielding commitment to protocol is necessary for a researcher. But for a doctor? For a human being? My willingness to abandon my experiment is not a lack of scientific discipline. It's a recognition that the unusual physician's calling to which I referred at the top of this letter had been set suddenly before me. I recognize that the only cure for the girl's ailment is a decidedly nonmedical one: discover the truth of how she'd come to be institutionalized. Find the actual killer. Correct this miscarriage of justice. I want you to know that however this endeavor comes out, I believe I am in the right place for the right reasons.

"Whistling to keep up courage is no mere figure of speech," you wrote in *The Principles of Psychology*.

Well, I have been whistling from the moment I arrived in Sunbonnet.

So far, it's working.

To all appearances, Sunbonnet could be any of a thousand prairie towns.

Nothing about this picturesque prairie town puts one on guard. Stately trees line the wooden sidewalks of Main Street. There's a row of brick buildings with a dry goods store, bank, post office, cigar stand, and butcher shop. The opposite side of the street has a general store, livery, the blacksmith and machine shop, the schoolhouse, and a pristine clapboard church and hall. Set among these buildings, on either side of the street, are a few dozen small wooden houses with neat yards and gardens behind whitewashed picket fences.

At one end of Main Street is a squat train depot to which I was delivered from Topeka; at the other end is the Peabody Hotel, twelve rooms in a three-story brick building with surprisingly up-to-date furnishings. The Peabody has a modest saloon that is as respectable as any drinking establishment can be. A less reputable saloon catering to farm hands and rowdies can be found on Green Street—nothing more than a dirt road. Of the saloon downstairs I can report this much: it's quiet enough to provide no impediment to my concentration on this letter. My single complaint is that the other registered guests here are strutting salesmen, from Missouri, Ohio, or Illinois, who made far too much of my simply strolling through the lobby and dining room. These grinning hawkers are nothing more than cigar-stinking nuisances, though when they leer, I have an impulse to punch their mustachioed faces.

Immediately outside town, the main road narrows in both directions to rutted lanes that stretch as far as the eye can see, through well-planted prairie and the forty or fifty family farms that surround the town.

This is the lay of the land. And I am here.

Allow me to summarize what I accomplished before leaving Topeka.

I visited the Kansas Hall of Records and the offices of the Bell Telephone Company and found relevant information in each. I also telegrammed my dear cousin Frank, a Chicago newspaper reporter who was dispatched to Sunbonnet two months ago to cover Dorothy's legal hearing. His reporting never made it to print, as his editor thought the legal settlement anticlimactic. It was Frank who suggested I meet the girl, as he noted parallels between Dorothy's recollections of magical figures and my work with emblematic images found in hallucinations and dreams. Neither Frank nor I imagined my work with the Gale girl would be anything but academic. But now this . . . From Topeka, I wired to request his notes, which arrived there three days ago. His observations inspired in me a number of questions about the hurried and ill-conceived outcome of Dorothy's case, questions that have since weighed heavily on my mind.

The most important of these questions is this:

Much of the case against Dorothy relies on her confession to having "melted" a witch during the period when Alvina Clough was desecrated in a like fashion. What could explain the confluence of the girl's statement with the woman's death? Unlikely coincidence? Or did Dorothy actually commit the crime? A thorny problem indeed and sufficient to get the girl locked away. Even before I visited the Kansas Hall of Records and the offices of the Bell Telephone, I knew that finding a solution is fundamental to mounting any post-judicial defense of the girl. Absentmindedly thumbing through the Tarot cards whose imagery I use in my practice, I realized there exists a third possibility to explain the otherwise damning circumstances. Reviewing the judicial testimony, I formulated a new timeline of events. The twister wreaks havoc and Dorothy disappears; then Dorothy reappears in a pumpkin patch, with no viable explanation; she relates to the town doctor her otherworldly experiences in a place she calls Oz.

The next day, Alvina's body is discovered in her home, and Dorothy is tied to the crime. It is not difficult to understand why the common and immediate assumption would be that the brutal offense occurred during Dorothy's absence and that her reference to melting a witch was a thinly veiled recollection of her crime. But what if the dousing of the victim with a chemical corrosive occurred *after* Dorothy made her confession in the doctor's office? What if the desecration of the woman's face occurred *because* Dorothy had seemed to confess to such an act? What if the actual melting of the woman was a means of diverting blame away from the malefactor and toward an innocent girl?

But wait . . . I hear your voice, Professor James, and I know you have Occam's razor in hand.

"Why strain for an alternative explanation when a simpler one already exists?"

I understand that the most straightforward explanation of events is simply that Dorothy Gale committed the crime. I cannot yet refute that with evidence. But I have met the girl, and I do not believe her capable of such violence. Oh, I can guess what you are thinking now. How can I be certain of what violence Dorothy may or may not be capable of committing? I'd have the same question if I were reading rather than writing this letter. I understand your skepticism. After all, I was trained in psychology at your feet. I acknowledge your professional imperative to regard my unproven assertion of the girl's innocence as some sort of veiled reference to my own life. Don't we psychologists attempt to draw such parallels in our interviews with patients and regard their assertions about the world and others around them as disguised references to their own states of mind? But no. I am not your patient. At least not anymore. And I can say this much with certainty: I am *not* misattributing pacifistic characteristics to a violently deranged girl. Dorothy is as I perceive her to be. I am *not* asserting her innocence due to misplaced sympathies arising from my own circumstances: the psychiatric institutionalization and eventual suicide of my mother. I know you're thinking it. You are trained to think it. As am I. But that does not make it so. My mother's madness plays no part in my analysis of the situation here in Kansas. My mother came to a sad and bitter end, yes.

Does that mean that I must forever after be subject to psychological second-guessing in my own professional observations, analyses, and prescriptions of action? What freedom is there in that? Absent the freedom to come to my own conclusions, *I* might as well have been the one found hanging by the neck in that cold, dank room at the asylum.

"Methinks the lady doth protest too much"?

Perhaps I do protest too much.

Professor James, it's both a gift and a burden to have your distinguished voice in my head.

I'm no detective, but I understand that many criminal cases are solved by simply asking *cui bono*, who benefits? After the twister, Alvina Clough was not seen alive again by any townsfolk. Three days passed between the twister and the mustering of a small group of townsmen to call at her house, where, on the fourth day, they discovered her desecrated body. My supposition that the poor woman was doused with chemical corrosive only *after* Dorothy related her story in the doctor's office narrows the time period during which such a brutalization can have occurred. More significantly, it suggests that the desecration was undertaken to conceal, by misdirection, the identity of Alvina's actual killer, who knew that the body would be discovered sooner rather than later, and recognized the Gale girl's "confession" as a fortuitous opportunity. Cui bono? The murderer, obviously. Whoever he is, we know this much is true of him: today he exercises an unencumbered liberty that rightfully belongs to Dorothy Gale. Instead, the girl lives in virtual solitary confinement. Merely proposing an alternative scenario for the crime is not the same as securing Dorothy's freedom. It is obvious there's little sympathy among townsfolk for the poor girl. Her incredible recollection of Oz, replete with paganism and witchcraft, is held against her as evidence of moral corruption. It will be necessary for me to offer more than reasonable doubt to get her case reconsidered. I harbor no illusions. I must identify the killer if Dorothy is ever to be set free. And if Dorothy is not set free, then I don't know how I shall ever feel free myself.

Go ahead. Take that apart and put it back together in some psychological way if you like. I'm sure it reveals something of significance about me. I don't care. I mean it only as a statement of my commitment.

In the meantime, I have a crime to solve.

During the period between Dorothy's interview with the town doctor and the discovery of Alvina's body the following morning, only a handful of townsfolk had heard of the girl's claim she'd melted a witch. Within days, word of her "confession" spread like a prairie fire. Gathered in the office that afternoon were the doctor; Dorothy; and the girl's aunt and uncle, Emily and Henry Gale. No one else. These four agreed not to share *one word* of the girl's murderous claim. However, minutes after the Gales left, the doctor telephoned the reverend to warn him that the girl he was about to take into his home for protection and spiritual guidance could be a serious danger. This extended to four the number of townsfolk (excluding Dorothy) who knew enough during those critical hours to make devious use of the girl's account. But since the telephones in Sunbonnet are wired in a single circuit, there's a town-wide party line. Anyone with a telephone might have overheard Dr. Ward's warning to Reverend Richter and taken the nefarious action. At first, I considered this a catastrophe for my investigation, as it would seem to expand my list of suspects to an unworkable number.

Then I remembered the twister and considered what even a moderate nor'easter does to the telephone lines in a civilized town like Cambridge. So I visited the offices of the Bell Telephone Company in Topeka; there, I acquired repair records for Sunbonnet after the storm. Among the twenty-two telephones currently installed in the town, most in places of business, all but four were still in need of repair six days after the twister ripped the wiring loose. This means that on the afternoon Dr. Ward telephoned his warning to Reverend Richter, only two additional telephones were operational in the town. One belonged to the sheriff and the other to the mayor. Either man might have overheard the doctor's warning and used it as an opportunity to conceal the true nature of a crime he must already have committed. Or perhaps the doctor or reverend committed the offense. Or possibly even Uncle Henry or Aunt Emily . . . At this point, I cannot point to one over any other.

By the time my train pulled into Sunbonnet I'd made a list. It must be one of these six:

Dr. Edmund Ward
Reverend Ralph Richter
Sheriff Hugh Hutchins
Mayor Carson Watt-Smith
Henry and Emily Gale

As I disembarked the train a few hours ago, I don't know what the townsfolk thought of me.

I'm quite sure it was not this: I am a dangerous woman. But that's what I am.

Don't laugh, Professor James.

One needn't be Wyatt Earp to set matters right.

It was after five PM when I arrived, so I accomplished little this evening besides checking in to the hotel, unpacking my things, bathing to deterge myself of the dust that accompanies travel, partaking of a serviceable meal in the dining room, and writing this letter. I hope you do not mind my communicating with you in such detail. I find it useful to arrange my words on a page. It serves to organize and discipline my thoughts, to see past the impediments to my undertaking, and to feel less alone. You have always helped me in these ways. But enough about that. More tomorrow.

My best to you and your family,

Evelyn

P.S. Perusing these pages just now, I'm doubtful that I've fully captured my situation. I am somewhat proud of the deductive processes I began in Topeka. However, there remains much about events here that I do not know and, far worse, cannot imagine ever deciphering. I would feel a fraud if these pages suggested otherwise to you, Professor. I am no detective. I'm riddled with questions. Fundamental questions. Who are these people? What have they done? And why?

Who are we human beings that such terrible things as this happen? Who am I to believe I can rectify it when I've barely managed to pull my own life together these past few years? Of course, if I had the answers, I'd never have come here from Topeka. Rather, I'd have given the poor girl in the insane asylum everything she needs to escape that place, grow up properly, and live her life. But I have no solutions for her. I am here now to ask questions. Nothing more, really. Perhaps I'm not so dangerous after all. But I am here.

Chapter 12

Regarding the events of September 1896

Sunbonnet, Kansas

We had no inkling of the out-of-town journalist's fateful letter that he sent to his female cousin just before he and the other unruly hacks departed our town. It would be more than a month before we learned of the missive, and by then it was too late to avert its consequences. While we never actually read the letter, we came to understand it had been written and posted immediately after the Gale girl's hearing by the newspaperman who had come all the way from Chicago. He is a luxuriantly mustachioed man of forty years named Frank Baum; the correspondence was addressed to his younger cousin, a female alienist (*psychologist* in the latest parlance) who lives in Boston or New York or some other citadel of sin. Her name was Dr. Evelyn Grace Wilford, and as she would eventually explain to us, her cousin Frank had written to her because he thought she might take a professional interest in the girl's bizarre tale. This is why: the Wilford woman's recent thesis extolled the virtuous possibilities of developing what she described as "a new psychological technique involving serious, thoughtful consideration of whatever mythological or fantastical imagery may be found in a psychiatric patient's dreams, hallucinations, or other fabrications."

In short, a brash, fruitless, and ill-advised academic exercise. Later, in an unguarded moment, she acknowledged that her thesis was considered disreputable by some in her scientific community and potentially embarrassing even by the slack standards of her fancy university and her overly permissive supervising professor, the world-famous Doctor Somebody-or-other. Her shoddy academic logic eluded us townsfolk, and we liked it that way. We value our sanity and our morals in Sunbonnet. The nearest we ever came to grasping her radical proposals was to consider them akin to taking *Bullfinch's Mythology* seriously rather than simply recognizing the tome for what it is, a phantasmagoria of stories from a childish, pre-Christian age. Why would one even *want* to take paganism seriously in our modern era? Excluding the diabolical, there can be only one answer: foolishness.

What were we to make of this Dr. Wilford, who traveled halfway across the country because she regarded the Gale girl's "memory" of Oz as meaningful? Was she diabolical or foolish? Being a generous people, we initially gave the lady doctor the benefit of the doubt. Foolishness. While that is clearly the lesser of the two evils, it is still a harsh judgment for a woman of fine education and a certain prominence. But recall it was not Alvina's murder or the subsequent legal proceedings that drew the Wilford woman to the girl's asylum and thence to Sunbonnet. Rather, it was this mythological balderdash. A heedless pursuit, reflective of a heedless woman.

For who but a heedless woman would spend her time and considerable personal expense on the Gale girl *after* the child had been committed to the state asylum and was thereby fully and permanently accounted for? The Wilford woman set aside her interest in fairy stories to focus on questions regarding Alvina's murder and the Gale girl's entanglement. To understand the disconcerting way things finally turned out, you must bear in mind the radical and morally irresponsible worldview that initiated the lady doctor's unsolicited involvement in our tight-knit and God-fearing community—In short, how she brought our town a uniquely dangerous brand of scientism wed to paganism.

CHAPTER 13

September 13, 1896

Dear Professor James,

It's the end of my first full day in Sunbonnet.

Allow me to start at the beginning:

This morning I awoke refreshed and in short order acquainted myself with some of the townswomen; I accomplished this by browsing for over an hour in the dry goods store (*loitering* might be a more accurate description) and then by taking the air in the newly planted square that passes for a civic park. Half the ladies I encountered looked upon me with immediate suspicion, as my appearance and manner gave me away not only as an outsider but, worse, as an easterner of some formal education. The other half seemed to overlook these suspect qualities. Naturally, they inquired why I was here. I thought it imprudent to acknowledge the true aim of my investigation, and I admitted only to my original objective in leaving Boston and coming to Kansas: to develop for scientific use a detailed psychological profile of the town's former resident, Dorothy Gale. I explained that whatever they could tell me about the girl and her upbringing would be helpful. But talk of a "murderess," even coming from a physician like myself, is no ordinary way to enter into cordial companionship.

Many of those who'd welcomed me terminated our conversation at the first mention of Dorothy and drifted away, grumbling about their laundry, children, the chickens. Others persisted in my company until I brought up Alvina Clough. Then they too exited, hissing among themselves. The remaining townswomen, while talkative, shared little useful knowledge of Alvina. How had the woman lived her entire life here and left so little of herself behind?

The townswomen expressed no sympathy for her years of solitude, but only for her painful and unusual death. The most energetic reminiscence of the poor woman came from Mrs. Humphreys, the druggist's wife, who took me aside and spoke in whispers. I listened politely as she described awakening from a deep sleep two nights after the twister. She's a chronic insomniac—nothing unusual about that. She climbed out of bed for a drink of water, glanced out the window, and caught sight across the deserted street of a black-clad spectral spirit kneeling outside the church door. After a moment, the figure, who she later came to believe was Alvina Clough's disembodied spirit, rose and disappeared into the darkness. A damned soul unable to enter the Lord's house . . . The instinct for the uncanny is strong everywhere, but in a town like Sunbonnet it's spoken of in whispers. The tale was lyrical and macabre but of no practical use except as a contrast to the colorless reality of the late unlamented Alvina. Still, Mrs. Humphreys believes it. I thanked her. Who knows how chronic sleeplessness and shocking news of violence might have affected Mrs. Humphreys?

As for Dorothy, these same women proved eager to share their observations. Just like residents of Fall River, Massachusetts, may still brag about having known Lizzie Borden when *she* was a girl. These observations were either so general as to be useless or so infected by the already growing mythology of Sunbonnet's most infamous resident that I couldn't be sure if they were describing Dorothy Gale or Belle Starr. I didn't give much credence to their testimony, so I include none of it here. I'm sure I needn't elaborate on this exclusion to you, Professor James. After all, it was you who wrote, "The art of being wise is the art of knowing what to overlook."

The one exception to the fruitlessness of these interviews was Mrs. Elizabeth Richter, the reverend's wife. I'd planned to call later at her home. She happened to be among those shopping at the dry goods store. She is a petite, fine-featured woman in her late forties and wears her graying hair in a conservative sweep up from her long neck, which certainly must have been a graceful and alluring feature when she was young. Her speech is unhurried and delivered with intelligence and impressive erudition. My guess is that her husband's congregation loves her; she seems born to be the wife of a public man. When I explained my interest in Dorothy, she touched me sweetly on the arm and volunteered to walk me about the town and introduce me to anyone who may be helpful to my inquiry. I needed no introductions, as I'm able to introduce myself when necessary. But I accepted her generous offer as it assured a reasonable privacy for our conversation.

We stepped out of the store and onto the board sidewalk, which runs perhaps a hundred yards along either side of the hard-packed dirt of Main Street. A group of women were gathered outside the dry goods store, admiring a baby in a pram. Mrs. Richter greeted them kindly, and they returned her warmth. We made our compliments to the child's mother and continued on our way. Only after we had moved out of hearing distance did Mrs. Richter return to our subject. "I'm sure you understand that Dorothy's arrival in our house was quite unusual."

Yes, I'd heard that the Richters had taken in Dorothy only hours after the girl's unexplained return to Sunbonnet. They'd cared for her through the dramatic weeks that followed and up to the afternoon of her transport to the asylum. I knew too that she and her husband had been the only townsfolk (including kin) who had made the trip to Topeka to visit Dorothy, albeit briefly. "Such tragic circumstances," I offered.

"Tragic . . ." She weighed the word. "To be honest with you, Dr. Wilford, when Dorothy arrived in our care, we didn't yet know about poor Alvina's demise. We found out soon enough. But that first day all we knew was the girl said something about 'melting a witch.' Since it was just one of many weird things she raved about, we never thought she'd actually done such a thing."

I could tell this was no time to argue Dorothy's innocence.

"Besides, I don't know if *tragic* is a word I'd choose," Mrs. Richter said. "Even knowing what we know now."

"Why is that, Mrs. Richter?"

"Please don't misunderstand me. The events surrounding the killing were certainly sad. Shocking even. Terrible. But when I think of *tragedy*, I think of Shakespeare and the classics. Of a hero undermined by a tragic flaw. The outcome is inevitable, no matter his efforts or intentions. And that's all well and good for drama. When it comes to real life, though, I subscribe to a more biblical perspective."

"And what is that?"

She stopped on the board sidewalk. A pair of round ladies gossiped across the street while a buckboard kicked up dust as it passed by. She nudged nearer to me and lowered her voice. "Let me be entirely honest. When it comes to the matter of predestination, I'm less aligned with Calvin and more with Wesley. A literary sort might view this as inevitability, tragic or otherwise. You see, I believe that one of the Good Book's greatest strengths is the hope it holds out for everyone. Yes, we are all sinners in the hands of an angry God, but grace will deliver us. Any of us. At any time. Tragic flaws notwithstanding."

"Dorothy too?"

"Of course." We resumed walking. "I don't often have the opportunity to discuss matters like this with a woman as well educated as you. It's a pleasure. I hope you don't feel I'm being self-indulgent."

I was impressed—and rather intrigued by Mrs. Richter too.

"Will you please keep this conversation between just the two of us?" she said. "My husband is a God-fearing man and a mighty spiritual leader. But I do not share all of his views."

"I look forward to meeting him."

"He's brilliant. And not just when it comes to theology. He studies everything. He's much beloved here." Once more she glanced around, not wanting to be overheard. "But if you want the truth, I'm not sure townsfolk fully appreciate him. I don't know if they grasp all the knowledge and learning he brings to the pulpit."

"Did you meet him here?"

"In Sunbonnet? Heavens, no. My father was a professor at the seminary in Indianapolis. My husband was his student. One evening, my father brought this handsome protégé home for supper. We were sweet on each other from that first night and married within months. Then we came back here, his hometown. That's going on thirty years now. Many lovely memories."

"Children?"

"We were never blessed."

"But you got to know Dorothy?"

"Yes. Maybe not as well as my husband. He'd spend three or four hours every afternoon discussing the Lord's ways with her. She is a very bright girl, but she didn't take strongly to his efforts. What would you expect? The girl has wandered off the path. Quite far off the path of righteousness. There's no sense denying it. Still, she's a good example of why I think none of us is beyond hope of ever finding God's grace."

"May we speak openly, Mrs. Richter?"

She smiled. "I thought we were."

"Knowing Dorothy, do you truly believe she's capable of committing such a heinous crime?"

Mrs. Richter stopped once more. "If not Dorothy, who else would have done it?"

That's what I hope to find out, I thought. *That's why I'm here.* But I said nothing. I felt comfortable enough with the woman, but I knew too little about the workings of Sunbonnet to share the true aim of my visit with anyone. Besides, her husband was on my list to interview. So I merely shrugged. "It's so disturbing."

"Yes." Mrs. Richter took a thoughtful breath. "Just as I believe grace may save anyone, I also believe anyone is capable of unspeakable evil should they come under the influence of the Great Deceiver. It works both ways, or it doesn't work at all. Don't you agree?" She didn't wait for an answer. "But what do I know? I'm just a minister's wife. I'm no 'consulting detective.' Are you?"

Both the question and the characterization took me aback. "Me?"

"Isn't that a charming thought? A woman detective! Don't you find that playful?"

"Oh yes, very." I smiled coldly.

"Sadly, this isn't a very playful town. But I do love it. The town, I mean. Home is home, after all. Gracious, look where we are."

We'd made a full circuit of the main street business district and were back at the dry goods store.

She held out her hand. "It's been a pleasure, Dr. Wilford. Please call on me anytime I can be of assistance."

There we parted.

I was left wondering: Am *I a detective or just playing at something?*

You're wondering that too, Professor James. I know you are.

I suppose we shall see.

As it was nearly midday and I was little farther along than I'd been upon awakening, I revised my plan for the day. I'd originally planned to speak with Dorothy's aunt and uncle. But since they lived outside town, I began instead with the four townsmen I think of as "the quartet."

As I write this, some hours have passed.

I've spoken to the doctor, the sheriff, the reverend, and the mayor. Allow me to relate my interviews with these four men. I think of them now not as a quartet, but as a *quadrumvirate*, an old-fashioned word that better suits them, as it seems to me ripe with menace.

DR. WARD

I began at the office of Sunbonnet's doctor, Edmund Ward. It made sense to start there, I reasoned. By doing so I might identify myself in the eyes of the town as a selfless Samaritan like Clara Barton, consulting on a matter of medicine, and not a threatening cosmopolitan like Irene Adler, operating on a secret agenda. Adler's a character in a Sherlock Holmes story . . . have you read it?

I can't say as yet how well the ruse worked. Not well, I suspect.

"It's a pleasure to meet you, Dr. Wilford," he said, rising from behind his desk as I entered the private office of his small medical practice.

"*Enchanté.*" I placed my hand in his. I was unsure then, as I remain unsure now, why I resorted to speaking French just then. It was the last sort of impression I'd intended to project. I hadn't planned it. Perhaps Dr. Ward's dark, deeply set eyes, white mustaches, well-trimmed Van Dyke beard, high collar, and cravat conjured an image of Hugo or the aged Delacroix. Being more nervous in my endeavor than I wanted to appear, I may have replied automatically, succumbing to mere association rather than method or deliberation. I instantly knew that I must be more composed with the others if I was going to accomplish my task.

"*Parlez-vous français?*" Dr. Ward asked.

"*Oui.*"

"Well, that won't get you very far around here," he answered. "Sit down, my dear."

If I was going to err, it felt fortuitous that I'd done so with Dr. Ward. He seems to possess in ample measure an inborn, reassuring bedside manner. I understood immediately why townsfolk trusted him (although our conversation did take a few acrimonious turns). Is a man who possesses such a gift for empathy capable of being a coldly calculating murderer? I rule no one out.

"You've come a long way, Dr. Wilford."

"Yes, it's been a fascinating journey."

"Please tell me what you saw."

"Saw?"

"On the train coming west."

I mentioned the endless miles of ripe wheat, flowering pastures, pale yellow cornfields, wilting oak groves, country towns, brilliant skies, gold ribbons of sunflowers stretching across the prairie, and entire counties that had been stripped bare and were now as gray as sheet iron.

"Do you travel, Dr. Ward?" I asked.

"It's been a decade since I traveled more than thirty miles from this spot." He straightened papers on his desktop. "Accident, illness, and misadventure do not take time off in Sunbonnet. So I'm rarely able to do so either."

"It's a demanding profession, Dr. Ward."

"It's my job. And what precisely is your job, Dr. Wilford?"

I summarized my research and subsequent interest in quintessential elements of the otherworldly story that Dorothy claims as truth. I clarified the question that drove my thesis: Might elements or characters from a patient's dreams or hallucinations provide coded but sublime clues to the deepest quarters of a patient's mind? I didn't go into detail. Dr. Ward expressed great interest in the psychological aims of my work. While he is not cognizant concerning recent developments in the field, particularly those of the past decade, he shows a professional interest in human nature. This was evident when he accurately described his former patient Dorothy Gale as being far brighter than average, with a degree of self-possession and confidence quite unusual among her peers. He also thinks her capable of tenderness, which he'd seen her heap upon her pet dog, Toto. I was pleased Dr. Ward acknowledged more than the locals' bogeyman characterization of the girl.

"Did you ever treat Dorothy for a serious illness?" I asked.

"Nothing out of the ordinary." He tapped a file on his desk. "She's always been a healthy girl. Physically."

"Physically. But mentally?"

"I think recent events answer that question."

I did not agree. So I said nothing and managed to conceal any pique or umbrage. You'd have been proud of my uncharacteristic discretion, Professor James. It was too early in the conversation to alienate Dr. Ward, as I occupy no official capacity. He could have asked me to leave his office at any moment. So I redirected him. "Did Dorothy ever demonstrate indications of hallucinations or other unusual mental phenomenon?"

"No. Nothing of that sort. Not until after the twister. Of course, she may have suffered such things, and I was never informed. Her aunt and uncle aren't the most reliable of guardians."

"No?"

"They raised a murderous blasphemer. Or is it a blaspheming murderess? Either way, need I say more?"

Again, I contained my irritation. "By all means."

"I suppose hindsight is crystal clear." Dr. Ward said. "The truth is I never noted anything unusual in the way the Gales raised their girl. Emily did her best. She's taken things hard. When it settled in on her just what kind of child she'd raised, she suffered a mild stroke a week or so after the twister. Her condition may have worsened since then. She doesn't show herself around town, and Henry's not allowed me to consult at their farm. Poor woman."

"And what sort of parent was Henry?"

"Henry never had much use for the girl, but he's hardly to blame, being understandably distracted all these years trying to make something of his hardscrabble property. It hasn't been easy on him. The only time we see him anymore is when he comes into town to frequent the saloon. Even when he's drunk, he hasn't much to say. Nobody presses him. He's quiet, but not like a stream or a field. More like a volcano fixing to blow."

"I understand it was you who urged the Gales to take Dorothy to the home of the reverend and his wife. Why?" Dr. Wilford asked. "When there wasn't yet any hint of a crime."

"I'd have thought that was obvious, Dr. Wilford, crime or no crime. The girl was skating on thin ice, spiritually speaking. Who is better prepared to deal with such matters than a minister? Also, I know Mrs. Richter to be a kind and nurturing woman. Childless, but maternal of spirit. I have no doubts about my recommendation in this regard."

"I met Mrs. Richter. She seems much as you describe her."

"Is there anything else?"

I was far from finished, but I didn't feel ready yet to launch into my more provocative questions and so chose to remain a moment longer on ordinary medical grounds. "So there was never any kind of medical issue for Dorothy? She never took a fall? No broken bones to set or lacerations to sew?"

"Nothing." Then something occurred to him. "The girl's colorblind. Her schoolteacher discovered it when they were painting pictures of flowers. Dorothy couldn't tell the difference between stems and petals. So the woman brought her to me, full of foolish hope that I could do something about it. As if there were some kind of cure . . . I remember it to this day because colorblindness is unusual. Particularly for a girl. Very rare, actually."

"Dorothy mentioned it."

"It's no day-to-day handicap. Nothing to disrupt a life. I'm surprised she mentioned it to you at all, given the more pressing matters she has to address."

"She brought it up to me because in this *other* place, Oz, she claimed she could see colors as never before," I answered. "But when she returned to Kansas, she once again lost the ability to tell red from green."

"Interesting how she incorporates an actual condition into her delusion. But you're the psychologist, Dr. Wilford."

"What was her condition when she arrived in your office?"

"You mean after the tornado? Remarkably well, actually. Perhaps a bit dehydrated. Nothing more. Which was suspicious in itself."

"Suspicious? Of what?"

He stood up, put his hands in his pockets, and walked toward the window. He glanced out and then turned back to me. "Her good condition suggested that she'd not spent the days and nights since the twister wandering alone around the countryside."

"She never claimed to have been wandering the countryside."

"I know where she *claims* to have been."

"And what do you make of it?"

"Her claim? You can't be asking me if I believe it."

"Of course not. I'm asking what, as a medical man, do you make of it?"

Dr. Ward turned again to the window, looking outside. He removed a handkerchief from his jacket pocket, leaned toward the window, and silently wiped a careful circle against a small smudge on the glass. His attention to the detail was striking. But the smudge proved to be on the outside, and so he sighed, frustrated, and returned the hanky to his pocket.

"Dorothy's claim, Doctor?"

"Meaning no offense to your psychological research, but . . . what is any sane person to make of such nonsense?"

"Are you referring to my research or to Dorothy's fantasies?"

"Dorothy's fantasies, I'd say."

"You're a sane person, Dr. Ward. So you can tell me. What *does* a sane person make of the girl's story?"

"Witches and wizard and talking animals . . . this whole Oz business?"

"Precisely."

He returned to the desk and shuffled his papers. When he looked up, he fixed me with an affable expression, almost as if he were an old friend. Or better yet, a mentor. "You're a bright and well-intentioned woman, Dr. Wilford. I suspect your research holds promise. I'm sure we could have a fascinating conversation about the symbolic meanings of the beasts, unusual personages, and any other 'magical' elements in the girl's tale of her time in Oz. We might even arrive at insights regarding her character. But despite my regard for your new scientific approach, I fear we'd only be wasting our time. At least in this instance."

"Why?"

"The girl's story didn't come from as deep a place in her mind as you speculate."

I didn't understand his objection.

"Let me be clearer." He placed his palms together and held them before his lips as if praying or, worse, attempting to explain a complex concept to a child or simpleton. (My dear Professor James, you would be proud of how I suppressed my impatience with Dr. Ward and listened with apparent politeness.)

"You see, my dear," Dr. Ward continued, "I don't believe the girl was relating an actual 'delusion' but was calculatingly concocting a fairy tale even as she shared it with me."

"Dorothy, calculating?" I'd seen nothing of the like in my interviews with her. "Why would you believe such a thing?"

"I didn't recognize it at first. Like you, I assumed she was relating some sort of dream or nightmare stemming from a blow to the head during the twister. Had that been so, your modern analytical approach might prove worthwhile. But it was no dream, no delusion. You see, my view changed dramatically when, in this very room, I asked her for the name of the magic land to which she had been 'transported.' She said it was called Oz."

"I know what it's called. So?"

"Please, Dr. Wilford, turn around and look."

I turned and saw an ordinary bookshelf and a small filing cabinet against a wall. There was a closed door that led out of the private office into the hallway. I scanned the titles of the books that lined the shelves but they were what you'd expect to find in a physician's office. "What am I looking for, Dr. Ward?"

"The bottom drawer of my filing cabinet."

The top was labeled "A–N" and the bottom "O–Z."

"You see it?"

I did but said nothing.

"What is it you see?" Dr. Ward said.

"The drawer and the label."

He seemed quite enthused by his own cleverness. "I only noticed it after the girl was taken to stay with Reverend and Mrs. Richter. But surely it's no coincidence. Rather, it suggests the child is duplicitous."

"It could be a coincidence. After all, it's a perfectly ordinary place to split the alphabet."

Dr. Ward's eyes narrowed. "The issue is not whether the labels split the alphabet in a reasonable way. You know perfectly well what I'm getting at."

"I do. And I still say it *could* be a coincidence."

"Frankly, I'm surprised by you, Dr. Wilford. Since when is coincidence a tenet of the scientific method?"

"The scientific method does not preclude the casino at Monte Carlo or the card rooms and roulette parlors from here to San Francisco from thriving in the business of chance. Science and chance are not mutually exclusive."

"Very long odds. Perhaps not, though."

"If Dorothy was sitting in this chair when you asked your question, do you expect me to believe she turned to the wall and noticed the filing cabinet before responding?"

"She was sitting here in my desk chair. She had a direct view of the filing cabinet."

"Your chair? Why?"

"Because I thought it might cheer the poor girl."

"Do you think she willfully constructed the story? Are you suggesting she's some sort of spontaneous literary genius? An eleven-year-old Lewis Carroll or Robert Louis Stevenson?"

"I don't know that her wizard and witches rise quite to that level, my dear."

I could see he was enamored of his alphabetical deduction and unlikely to let it go. "Why wasn't this included in her file? Or in the records of her hearing?"

"Justice would not have been served if such a prejudicial fact had been presented to the court."

"Why?"

"For God's sake, my dear, you must see that it's preferable that the girl be considered mad rather than evil."

"Do you think she's evil?"

"If ever there was 'evil' committed in this town—" He came to an abrupt halt. "I'm only a country doctor. And I'm a Christian one at that. So I don't make judgments."

I gestured back toward the file cabinet. "They're only two letters."

"Yes, O and Z. Oz."

"When Mrs. Pendleton discovered the girl in her pumpkin patch . . . did Dorothy mention the name of the magical place then?"

"She gave no name to the place. Not until she was seated in my desk chair facing that file cabinet."

I said nothing, but I must have allowed doubt to cross my face.

"Dr. Wilford, I think we can agree that the Gale girl is where she belongs, a place where she can do no further harm."

I disagreed. But yet it wasn't time to give full voice to my doubts. "May we turn for a moment to this murder business?"

"That's been dealt with, Dr. Wilford. As a matter of law."

"As physicians, the crime affects our mutual patient," I said.

"The Gale girl is no longer my patient."

"I understand that. But I think you underestimate how much this murder business—"

He stepped over me. "Alvina Clough, you mean? 'This murder business' . . . I don't like your phrasing, Dr. Wilford. It's a shame to refer to the poor woman only by what befell her, don't you think?"

"I mean no offense. But since my professional interest lies with Dorothy, it's only natural that I'd approach the topic of Miss Clough in light of the violent act. I don't mean to diminish the victim. What can you tell me about Alvina Clough?"

"There's really not much to tell. She was a difficult and solitary woman of fifty or so years who, despite her prickly personality, did not deserve her fate."

"Was she your patient, Dr. Ward?"

"I attend to the medical needs of just about everyone in this town. But I didn't see a lot of Alvina. I guess it has been seven or eight years since I last treated her. She'd come down with a case of the grippe. High fever. Close call. Generally, though, she was strong as a horse."

"And her relationship to Dorothy?"

"None that I knew of."

"Yet she named the girl her benefactor."

"Well, there were some legal entanglements as far as that's concerned."

"I'm aware of that." While in Topeka, I'd visited a law library and learned of a statute called the Slayer Rule, which dictates that no person who murders another may benefit financially from that crime. Now, although Alvina Clough was not nearly as wealthy as townsfolk assumed, the modesty of her estate was not publicly known until close to two weeks after her death. The inane and altogether unsupportable rationale that inheritance may have motivated Dorothy's crime had been used against the girl. Sitting in the law library, I considered the Slayer Rule's resultant legal disqualification of Dorothy Gale as Miss Clough's benefactor. I asked myself, *Qui bono?* I consulted a copy of the will and learned that no individual benefitted; rather, the document named the entire citizenry of Sunbonnet, which Miss Clough's father had helped to found, as the secondary beneficiary. Men, women, and children. After repayment of personal debt, including a mortgage on Alvina's house that nearly exceeded its value, this bequest amounted to less than forty cents per person. Obviously, this line of inquiry did nothing to narrow the field of suspects. Nonetheless, the bequest was not without value as it raised one important question:

"Legal entanglements notwithstanding, Dr. Ward, why would Alvina have bequeathed her assets to Dorothy?"

"No one's arrived at a satisfactory answer to that."

"But it's strange, don't you think?"

"Alvina was a strange woman."

"Even strange people have reasons for what they do. Strange ones. But reasons all the same."

"You're the psychiatrist, Dr. Wilford."

"Yes, but you knew Alvina Clough."

He opened his hands as if to show he hid nothing. "I have no clue why she'd single out the Gale girl. Maybe Dorothy was kind to her. Maybe the girl opened a door for the woman or chose not to partake in name-calling with the other children or some small thing like that."

"Would a small act of kindness be so unusual?"

"Directed to Alvina, maybe so."

"That's sad."

"You didn't know Alvina Clough, but yes, it is sad."

I was silent for a moment, and Dr. Ward seemed to take that as the end of our interview.

"And if there's nothing else . . ." he started.

But I wasn't finished, so perhaps I changed the subject too abruptly. In any case, the tone of our meeting changed when I asked without preamble: "Did you perform the autopsy?"

His expression immediately hardened. "Why would I do that?"

"I thought it was common in the case of a murder."

He sighed. "This is a God-fearing community, young woman. You're not in New York City or Boston, where murders are routine. You're in Kansas. Yes, we plains folk are well acquainted with death. But that doesn't mean we've lost our basic human decency. I hope in time you'll come to appreciate that. Cutting open a body just to confirm what is quite obvious to even an untrained eye is considered sacrilegious around here."

Quite obvious? "What is the official cause of death?"

"Cardiac arrest."

"How could you be sure?"

"That her heart stopped? I'm quite sure. Even as a mere country doctor."

"What if her death was caused by the lye itself? Liquefactive necrosis of the upper gastrointestinal and respiratory organs resulting from incidental ingestion of the caustic substance, for example?"

"I see you've done a bit of research."

"Surprisingly, there's more than one fine library in Topeka."

"Ah, yet another reason for us Kansans to burst with pride."

"I mean no offense, Dr. Ward."

"Liquefactive necrosis of the upper gastrointestinal and respiratory organs may have caused the poor woman's heart to stop. Or it may have been shock from the burning of the flesh on her face. But what of it, either way? I hope you don't think this is some kind of mystery story. This is real. In the real world things are, almost without exception, simply what they appear to be. I'd have thought your medical training would have made that clear to you. What caused Alvina's death was the caustic liquid and more specifically the eleven-year-old girl who 'melted' her. Appropriate actions were taken. Justice served, humanely. Cardiac arrest? Why not? Do you think things would have gone better for the Gale girl if an autopsy had returned a finding of liquefactive necrosis of internal organs?"

"I don't see how things could have gone any worse for Dorothy."

"It could have gone worse."

I said nothing but waited.

"Look what became of that Pomeroy boy," he said after a moment.

"Who?"

"The fourteen-year-old murderer currently serving a life sentence in solitary confinement someplace back east."

"I don't read the *Police Gazette*."

"Given the subject of your research, perhaps you should. But that's not my point."

"What is your point?"

"Dorothy was put nowhere so hopeless and grim as a prison. From what I hear, the Topeka Asylum is quite lovely. New buildings. Well-maintained grounds. Almost like a college campus."

"Surely you understand that what it looks like and what it is are two different things."

"Surely you understand that she's not in solitary confinement in state prison."

"But . . ."

"But what?"

"I've been wondering about Alvina's hands."

"What about her hands?"

"If somebody threw any liquid at your face wouldn't you put up your hands to try and block it?" I demonstrated what I meant, throwing my hands in front my face. "That's instinctive. Yet there's no mention of Alvina's hands bearing chemical burns in any account."

"You don't put your hands up to block something you don't see coming. Poor Alvina couldn't have suspected what the Gale girl was going to do. The poor woman never saw it coming."

"That may be, but wouldn't it be natural to wipe furiously when a chemical is burning your face, thereby incurring secondary burns on the palms?"

"Unless the shock of the initial dousing caused immediate *cardiac arrest*." He got to his feet. "Any other questions?"

I stood to go. "I may have a few more as my research continues."

"How long do you plan to stay in Sunbonnet?"

"Just a few days."

"Tomorrow night's our Wednesday Bible meeting. In the church hall. Most everyone turns out. Perhaps I'll see you there."

He showed me out of the building.

The interview was passably productive. It was different from the interviews I conduct with patients, my aim in those instances being therapeutic rather than investigative. Dr. Ward is not my patient. Neither is he a sympathetic colleague. Rather, he managed to be at once neighborly and antagonistic. Patients, too, can take oppositional positions. I'm familiar and quite comfortable with incorporating conflict into my work. Yet even in such instances there remains between doctor and patient a shared understanding that, whatever our differences, we're bound together in pursuit of the same goal—to get to the bottom of the pain. This sense of shared mission did not develop between Dr. Ward and me. Perhaps I pressed too hard on the question of the autopsy. Or the murder victim's unburned hands. In any case, I can tell Dr. Ward disapproves of my being here. And he's not alone in this. My interview with him was the first of three sessions today—in which the other townsmen who constitute the quadrumvirate imparted to me *their* various disapprovals. Nothing threatening. Nor even rude.

But as I reflect upon my time here, I'm reminded of a warning from a southern friend: "If they say to you, 'Well, bless your heart,' you can trust that they mean quite the opposite." Kansas is not the South. But the spirit of the warning seems to hold true.

Allow me to remain on the topic of Dr. Ward one moment longer . . . Do I think him guilty of malice? Or murder?

Does the doctor's failure to conduct an autopsy on Alvina Clough represent a conspiratorial act, or is this simply the way things are done around here? I shouldn't assume evil intent in everyone I meet. But it might be a prudent starting point. While I learned nothing conclusive from Dr. Ward, I gained a clear sense of how the town would perceive my presence: cautiously and defensively. And I knew that Dr. Ward, a man of science, is likely to prove among the *least* resistant (unless he *is* the villain). So, as I crossed the dusty street from the doctor's rooms to the small office of the town's sheriff, Hugh Hutchins, I resolved to be more subtle.

Apparently, I fell short in this effort.

SHERIFF HUTCHINS

"Is the sheriff in?" I asked a towheaded boy of about twelve, who sat with his feet up on an uncluttered desk, a week-old newspaper spread open before him. The room was otherwise deserted. The boy muttered something I didn't catch, as I'd become distracted by what struck me as an oddity of the office. Turning in a slow circle, I spied no "WANTED" posters tacked to the walls, no rack of Winchester rifles ready for grabbing by deputies responding to a riotous incursion of drunken cowboys on horseback. And there was no dangerous, wisecracking bank robber locked up in the single jail cell at the far end of the room—the empty six-by-nine-foot cell was neatly kept, like the rest of the office, and complete with washstand and metal pitcher. Instead, amateurish oil paintings of farm landscapes hung on the walls. Most disconcerting to me was this: the place smelled neither of fear nor horses, but of freshly baked pie. Aside from the iron bars on the cell, this room might have been a schoolmarm's study. Has everything I've read about life on the western plains been a lie? I was relieved by the tidiness and good order of the place, but I was also a bit disappointed. I asked the boy to repeat what he'd said.

He ignored me.

"Is the sheriff in?" I repeated, louder.

He nodded.

"May I see him?"

He looked up at last, almost comically world-weary for one of such tender years. "You in some kind of trouble?"

"No," I said.

"Then maybe the sheriff isn't your man."

"I just have a few questions."

"Such as?"

"Look, young man, is the sheriff in or not?"

The boy sighed, then shouted: "Sheriff, somebody here to see you."

After a moment a door opened, and Hugh Hutchins emerged from a storage room.

"Sheriff Hutchins, I presume?"

He ran his hand through his hair. "Ma'am?"

Tall and barrel-chested with heavily lidded eyes and a well-trimmed mustache, he moves gingerly, as if his joints are riddled with rheumatism, though he can't be much over forty. This prairie sheriff wasn't dressed in Western attire, dusty from chasing outlaws on horseback. Instead, he wore a clean business suit with vest and watch chain. He looked more like a homespun Bat Masterson than Wyatt Earp. I wondered if he'd ever drawn a gun, which, incidentally, did not hang from a belt slung low on his waist, as I'd expected, but was nowhere to be seen (even the Cambridge police carry guns).

"My name is Dr. Wilford."

"Ah, a lady doctor." A smile spread across his face. "Well, if that don't take the cake." Then he removed a tin star from his jacket pocket and pinned it on his lapel. "There we go. That's better now."

Perhaps I allowed an expression of mild disappointment to cross my face. Truly, what could be less relevant to a serious inquiry into the charges against Dorothy Gale than my childish preconception of what a Western sheriff should look like? I hadn't intended to share any such reaction. But judging from what Sheriff Hutchins said next, I must have done so.

"I'm sorry, Dr. Wilford," he said, opening his palms as if to indicate this was all the show to be seen. "We're not exactly in the Indian territories here. Maybe twenty years ago you'd have found a little more Western romance in these parts. Though that's not for certain. If you want that sort of thing, you'd be better off with a Bret Harte story or a Buffalo Bill Wild West Show. But . . . if you're looking for the sheriff of Sunbonnet, then you've come to the right place."

"I'm sorry. I didn't mean any disrespect."

"None taken. We all know our place here. We know what's required to make our town safe and happy. And what matters more than that? Nothing. Now, may I inquire, Dr. Wilford, as to your business with me? That is to say, what brings you here?"

For all his homespun self-deprecation, I found it hard to believe he'd heard nothing of my arrival. The town isn't big enough to keep news of the sudden appearance of an unaccompanied young woman, particularly a doctor from the East Coast who is asking questions about the town's painful recent events, from making its way to the sheriff. I found it hard to believe no one had informed the lawman of the interviews I'd conducted that morning in the guise of casual conversation with townswomen.

I chose instead to assume that Sheriff Hutchins's claim of ignorance regarding my arrival and activities must be an attempt to gain advantage. That Hutchins was no Wyatt Earp did not mean he was simple.

"Have you family in town?" he said. "Come for a visit?"

"I've come to ask a few questions about Dorothy Gale."

"Why would you want to do that?"

"Research. My medical specialty is psychology."

"You mean insanity and such?" Sheriff Hutchins said.

"That's part of it."

"Then I can understand why you'd be interested in the Gale girl." He shook his head. "Didn't know her. I just seen her from time to time like any of the kids around here. Never stood out as far as I could tell, one way or the other. And that's about all I can say on the subject. Wish I could be more help. I'd suggest you talk to her schoolteacher, but old Mrs. Franklin left town after they let her go from her position. She didn't leave no forwarding address. Sorry you wasted your time here."

I looked at the towheaded kid, who remained half hidden behind the open newspaper. "Did you know Dorothy?"

The boy lowered his newspaper lazily. "Me? Sure. I seen her plenty, but I didn't really know her. She's just a dumb girl." When he went back to his newspaper, I watched him closely for a moment. I couldn't tell if he was reading the newsprint or only pretending to.

"Sorry we can't be of more help to you," the sheriff said.

"I also have questions about Alvina Clough."

The sheriff frowned, then reached into his trousers pocket and tossed a nickel in the boy's direction. "Run up to the depot and buy me the paper."

"But we already got the paper. Right here."

"That one's a week old, boy," Hutchins said.

The boy folded the paper, set it aside, and snatched the coin from the wooden floor.

"Go," Hutchins insisted. "Now."

Coin in hand, the boy ran from the room and out into the street.

"What's his name?" I asked.

"Todd," the sheriff said. "Like the family name of President Lincoln's wife." He lowered his voice as if sharing a confidential thought. "I wouldn't make that particular historical allusion to just anybody around here, since there are still a few folks who don't take a liking to our sixteenth president. But seeing as you're from the Northeast, I know you'll take it in the right spirit."

"Is he your son?"

"Him? Naw. His mama was carried off by influenza when he was still in swaddling. His daddy, a good man who done the best he could in the years since, was struck by lightning in his tomato patch and killed a few months back. I took the boy in for the time being. He's got no truck with schooling. Can't read a lick. No talent for it. His looking at that newspaper when you walked in was just his way of being clever. The *Weekly Gazette* might as well be written in Chinese for all it means to him. So, seeing as his prospects are poor, I make work for him sweeping and cleaning my office here and the offices of a few other of the local grandees."

"That's kind of you."

"It's either this or the orphanage. Or maybe work as a field hand, but Dr. Ward says Todd's of too weak a physical constitution for labor, so there's no future for him in that. I'm hoping the boy takes to some kind of work that can see him through. He's not a bad boy. But I can't say it's been easy."

"My compliments to you."

"It's what folks do." He turned and indicated a pair of wooden chairs set beside an unlit potbellied stove. "Why don't we sit down here, and you can explain your business. The killing of poor Alvina Clough is put behind us, thank God. I hope you understand how much that took out of this town. So I'll be very interested in hearing what reason you have for stirring it all up again. I hope it's good, Miss Wilford."

"It's *Doctor* Wilford."

"It is?"

"I'm not here to stir anything up."

"Then why don't you tell me why you are here."

I gave the sheriff a greatly abbreviated explanation of my academic hypotheses.

He seemed to follow my approach to the psychological significance of the girl's "fantastical hallucinations," but soon his impatience grew palpable. He stopped me. "I don't really follow the difference between what you deep thinkers call *psychology* and what we ordinary folks call plain old human nature. But then I don't think my following your scientific arguments matters to you one way or the other, young lady." He leaned in toward me. "Am I wrong about that?"

"I'd prefer that you follow my line of thought."

"Maybe you shouldn't waste too much time and effort on that, and just tell me how I can help you. I'm a lawman.

Nothing more. Have you talked to Dr. Ward? Now, he's an educated gentleman."

"I just came from his office."

"Well then. I doubt I can add anything worthwhile to whatever he already told you, as far as helping with your doctoring project. Your *psychology*." He smiled. And almost looked friendly. "Yeah, the doctor's your best bet. I never made it past the fourth grade; you might be barking up the wrong tree here."

"You're a lawman."

"Yes, ma'am. I am that."

"Then you're exactly whom I want to talk to."

"Really." He shrugged. "Go on then."

"As a lawman, maybe you can tell me why an eleven-year-old girl would commit murder. I read through the transcript of the public hearing, and that question still nags at me. Why would Dorothy kill Alvina Clough?"

I hadn't intended to be quite so direct. The words just came out. But this is the truth: the four interviews I'd conducted this afternoon were nothing like the clinical situations to which I am accustomed. A life spent in libraries, hospitals, and wood-paneled seminar rooms may not be the best preparation for a criminal inquiry, especially when one hopes to keep secret for as long as possible the true aim of that investigation. In pursuit of this concealment, I failed rather quickly in all four encounters. But there are no text books on the subject, only fictions. And in the real world, having read Wilkie Collins and Arthur Conan Doyle turns out to be worse than no preparation at all.

"You're asking *why*?" The sheriff fixed me with an impatient, patronizing expression. "My job is more along the lines of figuring out *who* committed a crime, not why they done it."

"But I've been wondering about the element of motive in your investigation. Surely you take that into account."

He stared at me, expressionless. "When somebody steals a hat from the dry goods store, it's because they want the hat and don't want to pay for it. When there's a fistfight at the saloon that has to be broken up before one guy tears the hide off the other, it's because the gentlemen got their tempers worked up. And when a farmer plants fifty rows of corn on his neighbor's property, it's because he wants to increase his crop without paying for the land. It's not my job to dig deeper than that when it comes to . . . what's that word again? Oh yeah, *motive.*"

"But Sheriff Hutchins, those crimes are ordinary and entirely explicable. Rational, even. I'm asking about murder. There's nothing ordinary about that."

"You'd be surprised, Dr. Wilford. I began my career in Dodge City. And it was no Wild West adventure. But one thing the stories do get right about that miserable place is that life was cheap, and murder is as ordinary as shucking beans. And not one whit more interesting neither. Nobody ever had to ask why."

"I understand, but we're not talking about gunmen in gambling halls. We're talking here about a child killing an old woman."

"You got a point there, Doctor. If I'm completely honest with you, I guess I did ask myself once or twice why the girl would have done such a thing. I never bought that last-will-and-testament business. So I wondered. But then wiser heads got involved, and the girl was shipped off to the loony asylum and . . . well, after that you'd have to be insane yourself to keep asking why she done such a god-awful thing. The answer was put right in front of us at the public hearing. Madness. That's why she's at that asylum and why nobody in town's asking themselves the question 'Why?' It's madness. Plain and simple."

"Madness is never 'plain and simple.'"

"Guess that's why you're a doctor and I'm not."

He rose from his chair as if the interview was over. I remained seated because I wasn't finished. "I may have phrased my question wrong. I'd like to know if during your investigation you uncovered any previous relationship between Dorothy and Alvina Clough. I'm not asking whether they knew each other. Dr. Ward already says there's no indication they did. But did you find anything unusual that might indicate they were peripherally associated, maybe by a shared acquaintance or relative?"

"*Periphically?*" The sheriff tripped over the word. "Does that mean something like *indirectly*?"

"Right."

"This is a small town, Doctor. Everyone's connected in one way or another with everyone else."

"Even Dorothy and Alvina?"

He sat down and said nothing.

This was the first sign he might have something to share. I folded my hands in my lap and resolved to wait for him to speak next, regardless of any awkwardness in the ensuing silence. I use this technique from time to time with reticent patients. Of course, this is no revelation to you, Professor James, as I learned the technique in one of your seminars. You'll be gratified to know it worked.

After what *seemed* a full minute, the sheriff spoke. "There's one thing that struck me as somewhat unusual."

"Yes?"

"Didn't think much of it at the time, but after we discovered Alvina's body, I recalled it. Just a passing thought. But now that you ask . . ."

Again, I waited for as long as it took for him to start again.

"Well," he said at last, "the day after the twister, me and a handful of others were helping Henry Gale sort things out at his property. And I happened to notice that half buried in the wreckage of the house was a tiny cast-iron model of the Big Ben clock tower. You know, the famous one in London, England. 'Bout just this big." He indicated a space of about four inches. "It was mixed in with a few other items that belonged to the girl. Her Sunday shoes, her Sunday dress, a rain slicker, a baby doll, and the like. Now, you may be wondering why I'd find that peculiar."

"I am wondering."

"Some years ago, Alvina left Sunbonnet for the only time in her life. She went on a yearlong European tour. All the famous capitals. We knew she could well afford it, but it didn't seem much like her. She wasn't the adventurous type."

"She went by herself?"

"No, she met some aunt in Pittsburgh, and they embarked together out of New York Harbor. What surprised us even more than her going was that when she came home from her travels, she brought back a suitcase full of souvenirs. Small cast-iron models of the Roman Colosseum, the Leaning Tower of Pisa, and the Big Ben clock tower, like the one I saw in the wreckage of the Gale girl's room. She also brought back dainty lace handkerchiefs from Belgium and fine wool scarves from Scotland. And she passed them out as gifts. It was probably the only neighborly thing she ever did in her life."

"If she passed the souvenirs around, why were you surprised to see one in the wreckage of the Gale house?"

"I didn't say she gave one to *everybody*." He chuckled. "You obviously don't know much about Alvina. Or maybe it's that you don't know nothing about the Gale family. So let me give it to you straight. Alvina only gave those souvenirs to the pillars of the community. The mayor, the doctor, the reverend, the station master, and a few shopkeepers and other business owners. Had these souvenirs for their wives too, the hankies and scarves. But she had nothing for nobody else. Oh, *maybe* she'd have given a lace hankie or cast-iron model of Big Ben to one of the handful of wealthy farmers who come into town from time to time. Maybe they counted for something with her, even if they had callouses on their hands. But *wealthy* is not a word you'd ever use to describe the Gale family. Hardscrabble dirt farmers is more like it. That's why I took note of the Big Ben in the wreckage of the girl's things. I was surprised Alvina would have given the Gales the time of day, let alone a souvenir of Europe. Like I say, it was just a passing thought. Don't mean nothing."

"Did you ask Henry and Emily how the souvenir came to be there?"

"Nope. When I spied it in the wreckage, Henry was in quite a worked-up state, seeing as his house and windmill had just been destroyed and his niece was missing and presumed dead. So I let the matter lie. And, afterward . . . well, the whole thing slipped my mind, what with all the other things that came to light. When I thought of it again, it didn't seem important. Fact is, it still don't."

"Did Alvina give you one of the souvenirs, Sheriff Hutchins?"

He grinned widely. "I'm surprised you even have to ask. Let me put it to you this way. Do *you* consider the longtime sheriff to be a pillar of a community?" He didn't wait for an answer. "Fact is, she gave me one of the same Big Bens as I saw in the wreckage of the Gale house. I believe I still have it in my storage room." He started toward the door. "Let me show you."

"That's all right—no need." I'd seen such cast-iron reproductions of European landmarks before. "Did you note any unusual details about Alvina's death that might not have come up in the official hearing a few weeks later?"

He stopped mid-stride and turned a hard gaze on me. "I was a sworn officer at that hearing. If there was something unusual, you think I'd let it be overlooked? Are you questioning my commitment to justice?"

"Not at all."

"Or my competence?"

"No."

"Then what are you trying to get at, Dr. Wilford?"

The door opened, and the towheaded boy dashed inside with a fresh newspaper in hand. "I got it," he said, holding up *The Weekly Gazette*.

The sheriff glared at him. "Where's my change, boy? The newspaper's just three cents."

I was sorry for the lad, who couldn't know that he wasn't the true source of the sheriff's aggravation. Sheepishly, the boy produced two hard candies. "I got two penny candies, one for me and one for the lady," he said.

The sheriff took a deep breath. "You can give the lady a candy, seeing as she's a guest who's on her way out."

The directive was evident. So I stood with my bag in hand and stepped toward the boy. He placed a candy in my upturned palm. "Thank you," I said.

"Put that other candy in the trash, boy," the sheriff said. "Right now while I can see you." He loomed over the child. "You don't make decisions about how to spend *my* money without asking permission, you hear?" He didn't wait for the boy to answer, but turned to me. "You got to teach people respect, young people especially. Adults too. All kinds of people when you get down to it. Even those who should know better. *Respect.* Shouldn't be that hard to learn, but . . ." He shrugged and twisted the door handle to show me out. "You have a good stay in our town, ma'am."

And I was back on the street.

I hoped things would go better with the minister. But just as I got to the small church office, I was interrupted by the towheaded boy. Todd had slipped out of the sheriff's office and run to catch up to me at the steps leading to the door of the church office.

"Miss?"

I stepped back down to the road. "Well, hello, Todd. Did I forget something in the sheriff's office?"

"No. But I got something for you anyways." He opened his hand and there in his palm were two more candies. He smiled sheepishly. "Actually, they aren't a penny apiece, but *two* for a penny. The sheriff don't know the cost of things because he leaves all the shopping to Mrs. Hutchins." He extended the candies. "They're for you. One of them, at least."

I was of two minds about playing a role in the boy's deception of his guardian. No, that's not accurate. I was quite sure I ought *not* to indulge the boy's offer and, indirectly, his petty dishonesty. But his expression was one of innocent delight that would have been unimaginable on his face when I first saw him perched at the sheriff's desk, perusing a week-old newspaper he couldn't even read. Todd could have kept his secret candy cache all to himself, but instead he'd acted on a large-hearted impulse. And I thought of the harsh way his guardian had spoken to him. In any case, I gave the boy a brief, obligatory look of adult concern and then took one of the hard candies he offered and popped it into my mouth. "You're very generous," I said. Then I started back onto the road to respectability. "But it's important in the future that you always be honest with—"

"I'm honest, Miss," he interrupted. "I never steal nothing out of any of the offices I straighten up. I'm in one or the other of them at night, by myself mostly. But I don't never take nothing. Because I respect the men who give me work."

"How many offices do you straighten up?" I asked him.

"Besides the sheriff's?" Todd calculated a moment. "Five." He pointed up to the door at the top of the step. "The reverend's office right there, for one. He don't let me do much straightening up. Don't blame me for the mess you'll see when you go inside. And I clean the office of Mr. Hearn, the editor of the newspaper. And Mr. Garrison, the general store manager. And Mr. Watt-Smith, the mayor. And the doctor, who sometimes leaves sweets out for me. None of them ever got a bad word to say about me. You can ask. You won't hear one single bad word."

"You keep it that way, Todd." I smiled and turned to go.

"Miss?" He kicked at the sidewalk's boards with his battered boot. "I did know Dorothy. Better than I let on to you before. They don't talk about her no more, so I didn't feel right saying anything with the sheriff there. You understand?"

"I think I do."

"I got something to tell you about her. Something you should know."

"I waited a moment before prodding, "What is it?"

"She was nice. For a girl."

"Is that all?"

"That's a lot."

"Thank you for sharing that with me, Todd."

"She taught me how to write my name. All the up and down and across strokes. And the circles. For example, my name's a telegraph pole followed by a circle and two half circles that face to the right. She taught me how to write her name too. Her name is *much* harder to write than mine."

"I think she's nice too, Todd."

"Yeah." He twisted his lips in dismay and looked at the sky. "Too bad she's a murderer."

Before I could respond, the door to the church office opened, and out came Reverend Richter. He stopped a few steps above us. He's tall and sturdily built. His well-trimmed beard, lightly sprinkled with gray, cascades well below his collar. From high on his forehead, a wave of salted hair sweeps straight back, creating an unusual symmetry, a hirsute framing of his eyes, which are a shade of gray that rightfully can be called luminous. Such a striking appearance must be an asset in his profession.

"May I be of assistance?"

He must have peered out his office window and observed the boy and me at the foot of his narrow stoop. We hadn't been noisy enough to have alerted him otherwise. Therefore, thankfully, I think it unlikely he heard my ethically ambiguous acceptance of Todd's contraband candy. Still, his gaze made me feel like a girl caught out giggling or gossiping during a church service.

"Would you two like to come inside?" he asked, his manner amiable.

"Got to go, Reverend," Todd called over his shoulder, and rushed back in the direction from which he'd followed me.

We watched him go.

After the boy disappeared around the corner, the reverend said, "Children are a heritage from the Lord. That's what the Psalms say." He descended the steps until he stood beside me. "Todd's not a bad boy, but he's had a bad turn. Orphaned." The reverend's manner was earthy and reflective. "Sheriff Hutchins is a good Christian and took him in for the time being. The lad's blessed to be under somebody's roof. I assume you've met the sheriff?"

"Yes, just now."

"Then you know he's a fine man." He extended his hand. "I'm Reverend Richter. Welcome to our town."

I shook his hand. "Dr. Evelyn Grace Wilford."

"Yes, I heard about your being in Sunbonnet."

It was a relief the reverend wasn't playing ignorant to my arrival, as the sheriff had tried to do. "I had the pleasure of meeting your wife earlier this morning at the dry goods store. She is a bright and warm woman."

"Indeed she is. And Elizabeth had fine things to say about you as well."

I hoped she hadn't said too much. Somehow, I feared she'd seen through me. Was I being overly self-conscious? Did that even matter? By now everyone I'd met had likely seen through me.

"I understand why Dorothy would be of interest to you, a trained alienist," he went on. "She's had a fascinating life, especially to those of us who've known her since she arrived here as an infant. And for those like yourself, who don't know her as one of their own . . . well, hers is doubtless an intriguing *case*."

"She's more to me than a 'case,' Reverend."

"Really? I just spoke to Dr. Ward, who told me you had an academic interest in the girl's hallucinations. For your research."

"Yes, but she's still more to me than a mere subject."

"How long have you known the girl?"

"Not long. But gentle consideration and care require little time to develop."

"Very true, Doctor. Would you mind if I quoted you in my sermon this Sunday?"

"I'm sure you can find a more pious source than me."

"More pious?" He smiled. "I am always delighted and reassured by the humility of good people. Doctors, especially those who attend to children, as you do, often demonstrate such humility. Whether or not they know they're doing the Lord's work is less important, in the end, than the simple fact that they're doing it. I would be proud to quote such people from my pulpit all day long. Even if they weren't regular churchgoers. So I ask again: May I quote you in my sermon this Sunday?"

I nodded. "I imagine from your way with words that you're very good at your job." Born into other circumstances, he'd likely have become the rector of St. John the Divine or some other impressive institution. "Thank you for the compliment, Reverend. But I didn't come to discuss theology."

"I'm sure you have questions about our Dorothy Gale. Perhaps I can answer them. I hope so. Will you come inside?"

"Thank you," I said, starting up the steps, across the narrow porch, and in through the doorway.

He followed and closed the door after us.

REVEREND RICHTER

It was just as Todd had warned me. The reverend's study was a stark contrast to the orderliness of the sheriff's. I reminded myself again not to trade in expectations. Where I'd anticipated frontier ruggedness in the sheriff's place of business, I found instead a domestic fastidiousness suggestive of illustrations in a ladies' home magazine. Now, where I anticipated just such orderliness and comfortable furnishings, I discovered a chaotic jumble of books, papers, and framed prints in random piles about the floor. The room reminded me of many professors' offices I've been in. But not yours, my meticulous Professor James.

"Todd doesn't seem to do quite as much tidying up here as he does in the sheriff's office."

"He's a good enough boy," the reverend said. "No one would ever mistake him for a gifted student, poor fellow. But he keeps the other men's offices very neat. And I hope you'll note that this room isn't *dirty*." He ran the tip of his index finger on the windowsill. "See? No dust. The messiness is my doing. I have a system. I know where and how to find whatever I'm looking for. If this stuff were shelved and organized alphabetically, I'd likely be lost."

I found familiarity in the dishevelment. As you know, my own rooms on Beacon Street are similarly dominated by piles of books. Perhaps I was disarmed by it. And what the reverend said next reinforced my growing ease, for better or worse (worse, actually).

"I find your field to be of great interest, Dr. Wilford," he said, removing a stack of books from one end of a settee and motioning for me to sit. He remained standing. "That I am a man of the cloth does not make me an enemy of the scientific breakthroughs in your field of medicine. I believe foremost in the power of prayer. Nothing of Man's devising can ever be more powerful than the grace of the Lord. But I'm also aware, for example, of the value of sulfur, mercury, and copper as disinfecting agents in surgery or other medical procedures." He indicated the volumes piled on the floor. "Yes, my reading is primarily biblical, theological, scriptural, but there are other titles mixed in." He lowered his voice, looked around as if for eavesdroppers, and spoke in a stage whisper. "Even a few general science books, for example."

"Scandalous," I said.

"When I learned that you are an alienist, a student of the workings of the brain . . . well, I took your arrival to be a gift from the Lord. You see, my work involves, among other things, the counseling of my flock. All manner of human questions and experiences arise. And while the Bible contains all the wisdom necessary for any dilemma or circumstance, I believe there are techniques in your new field that may improve the communication of that wisdom to my flock, allowing me to be a better shepherd. Thus, my enthusiastic interest. Do you follow me, Dr. Wilford?"

"Yes. I can see how—"

But the reverend wasn't finished and continued speaking as if I'd said nothing. "Isaiah 38:21 states, *'Let them take a cake of figs and apply it to the boil that he may recover.'* Now, that's biblical. That's the word of the Lord. But if that isn't also a medical prescription, then I don't know what is. So you see, I'm not opposed to your work, Doctor. Nor is the Bible. However— having acknowledged this interest and sympathy—I must clarify my position regarding the *dangers* of your work."

"Dangers?" I asked at last.

"Shall I explain?"

What could I say but yes?

He lifted another stack of books from the settee and sat down, angling himself toward me and lacing his fingers together. "While I believe the willingness of you alienists—"

"We prefer these days to be called *psychologists*, if you please," I interrupted.

"As you will. I believe the willingness of you *psychologists* to listen without judgment to whatever the patient claims as truth demonstrates potential for better diagnosis and maybe even a degree of healing. But I also believe there are instances when a patient's claims must be noted for what they truly are."

"What they are?"

"Well, they're not mere delusions or hallucinations. Dr. Wilford, may I ask if you're a believer?"

"I was raised as a churchgoer."

My answer seemed good enough for him. "Then I'm surprised I have to clarify for you the true nature of the Gale girl's claims. "They're not mere indicators of a troubled mind, as are the hysterical claims of most of your patients, even the most violent. No, the girl's avowed 'memories'—extravagant as they may be—are of a different, nonmedical nature. Far more treacherous."

"And what is this 'nature'?"

"The girl's nature is diabolical, of course. The Bible is quite clear on the issue. In Leviticus it is written that '*A man or a woman who is a witch shall surely be put to death . . . their blood shall be upon them.*' You may ask, 'Why is the prescribed punishment so immediate and irrevocable?' And I would answer, 'Because witches and wizards are the most direct means by which Satan can enter into our minds, our hearts, and our souls.'"

Despite my earlier trepidation, I was further taken aback by the reverend's vehemence. "Even if I grant you that rather debatable assertion . . ."

"The Bible is not debatable," he said, raising his voice for the first time. "It is the Word of God. To believe otherwise is to be denied grace, or worse."

I had nothing to gain by debating theology. "Reverend, Dorothy never claimed to *be* a witch," I said, choosing this other, less confrontational tack. "She was terrified by the tornado and afterward merely recalled what may be thought of as a dream of being *among* witches, one of whom wanted to destroy her. That's neither here nor there as witches and talking beasts that reveal themselves in such ways merely stand for more tangible fears and threats in the real world. Indeed, my dissertation asserts—"

"No," he snapped. "That's where you go too far, Doctor. I'm generally sympathetic to your medical advances. And I hope I've already demonstrated that I'm no papal fanatic, burning heretics at the stake. But hear this clearly: witches do not *stand* for anything besides themselves. They're exactly what they appear to be—operatives of Satan."

"And those who relate tales of witches are diabolical too?" I said. "The Brothers Grimm, say?"

"Dorothy was not relating a *tale*, but something she claimed as real. Therein lies the difference."

"You can't be suggesting that her story is a literal account of events that actually happened."

"Of course not," the reverend said. "But such was *her* claim. And she never backed down from the prevarication. Doubtless, she was inspired by the Prince of Lies. If you allow yourself to take it all in . . . well, it is chilling. Good Christian minds, sanctified by the word of the Lord, are not likely to fall for any such diabolical maneuvers. The sanctified among us are not the Devil's primary targets. No, it's the weak he seeks to corrupt. Oh, if just one person were to take the girl seriously—"

"Be that as it may," I interrupted, "Dorothy never claimed to be a witch. Her most audacious claim was that she *killed* a wicked witch. She sits in an asylum now as a result of that claim."

"She's institutionalized because she killed Alvina. Let's not allow ourselves to be confused by the miasma of darkness that surrounds the girl's words and actions. The most damnably audacious claim she made was not that she had killed a wicked witch but that a 'good' witch had helped her in this faraway land. More than that, a good witch had saved her! *Good witch?* The words are right there as a warning to the righteous. This, even more than the crime of murder, is indelible evidence that the girl's soul has been overtaken by Satan and that she is now his instrument. We no longer stone witches. You're right—Dorothy's not herself a witch. She's merely a depraved killer of innocent women. And more damnably, she's a believer in 'good' witches. A dark prophetess shamelessly willing to share her message with anyone who will listen. Proverbs tells us that *'even a child makes herself known by her acts, by whether her conduct is pure and upright.'*"

I felt a new flood of empathy for the girl, beyond any that even the conditions at the Topeka Insane Asylum had inspired in me. "And this little girl lived with you for weeks?"

"Oh, I tried to dissuade her of this evil," the reverend continued, seeming to have missed my vitriol. "I spoke to her for hours every day. But she persisted. And now I fear only for the other inmates of the insane asylum who may yet be damned by their exposure to such a one as Dorothy Gale."

"And your wife?" I asked.

"What about her?"

"Does she feel this way about Dorothy?"

"She's a Christian woman."

I felt nearly defeated by his vehemence. *There are many ways to be a Christian,* I thought. But I didn't want to argue with the reverend. He'd hear nothing from me. I ought to have been better prepared. Perhaps his wife's cordiality had disarmed me earlier that day. I wanted to flee the room. But I knew that to race out now would seem a capitulation. I wouldn't give him that triumph.

"I can see by your face that you're taken aback," he said calmly.

"Somewhat."

"Good." Then he broke into a friendly, almost inviting smile. "The Lord's wisdom sometimes strikes us like a bolt of lightning. But do not despair. Proverbs also tells us, *'Let the wise hear and increase in learning, and the one who understands obtain guidance.'* Please don't take my words to mean only that I condemn the Gale girl, though I must. Please hear these words as a message of hope for you, Dr. Wilford. Hope that your soul may yet be saved."

My expression must have given away my discomfort.

"Dorothy is an intelligent and sometimes charming girl. I don't blame you, Doctor. I might have been taken in myself if Dr. Ward hadn't warned me of the girl's particular malice."

"Warned you?"

"Yes, on the day she turned up in Mrs. Pendleton's pumpkin patch. That was also the day my wife and I took her in."

"Warned you of what?"

"The filing cabinet. The 'O' through 'Z.'"

I said nothing.

"He told me the girl concocted the whole story. That her yarn was derived from no mere hallucination or dream, the contents of which might reasonably be considered beyond one's control, but was a bald-faced invention. Didn't he explain that damning detail to you?"

"He offered to me nothing more 'damning' than that his files are alphabetized in two drawers."

The reverend looked at me as if I were a child. "Let's not argue the fine points, Dr. Wilford. You may come to your own conclusions. This is a free country. But allow me to say this: I greatly appreciated the doctor's warning. Remember, the missus and I were taking this girl *into our home*. And if Dorothy was knowingly inventing details of this faraway land . . . well, you must see that this makes her praise for a 'good' witch that much more damning. The girl knows what she is doing." After a moment, he continued. "And that's not all the doctor warned me about that first day. You see, he was worried for my wife and me and felt we needed to understand just what sort of girl we were taking in."

"Dorothy is no 'sort' of girl."

The reverend chuckled. "Ah, doctor, you're obviously an educated and well-bred young woman, but I find it amusing that you still cannot rise above the emotionality of your sex. Please don't take that as a criticism. It's just an observation, and an affectionate one, at that. After all, Proverbs 31 states that *'many women do noble things.'* That is God's word. How can I feel anything but human warmth toward the emotional characteristics of your sex?"

Doubtless Proverbs 31 says many other, less admiring things about the place of women. But I reminded myself that I was here for information, not debate.

"Shall I continue?" he asked.

"We're speaking about Dorothy."

"Yes and about Dr. Ward's warnings."

I took a breath. "Please, go on."

"Very well." He pushed his desk chair around a pile of books, to narrow the distance between us, and sat down. He no longer loomed above me like a lecturer. "On that first day, no other townsfolk knew—outside of my wife, the doctor, and the girl's aunt and uncle—that Dorothy claimed to have *melted* and thereby killed a witch."

The reverend hadn't considered that Dr. Ward's message also might have been overheard by two other townsfolk on the party telephone line. I saw no advantage to telling him.

"Dr. Ward believed it was important we be told, though we agreed to share the detail with no one else. The mere claim was an abomination we didn't think the girl should have to bear in public. That night we locked Dorothy in her room to ensure our safety, a habit I maintained through the long weeks to follow. The next day, when Alvina's body was discovered *melted*, we could no longer keep the dark detail to ourselves. We had to share it with the sheriff and a few other important figures. The rest of the town learned about it soon enough. Ah, poor Alvina. What a terrible death. Our darkest fears about the girl were far, far exceeded."

His dramatic flair had grown repulsive, but I still had questions. "Why would the doctor warn you about Dorothy's claim *before* Alvina's body was discovered?"

Again, he looked at me as if I were a child. Perhaps, in retrospect, my question was foolish. "Any girl who claims to have committed murder, whether by 'melting' or by more ordinary means, is not someone to bring into one's home without warning. Dr. Ward was only doing the responsible thing. After the gruesome discovery, the melting of a human being . . ."

Dorothy's claim to have melted a witch remained at the heart of the matter. It might be just another detail of her hallucinatory fantasy to be interpreted as purely symbolic—that is, the "good witch" represents an idealized mother, while the "wicked witch" represents a malignant one, or some other such *prototype* à la Schopenhauer or *categorization* à la Kant. There remained the troubling fact of the desecration of Alvina's body, so symbolic explanations would carry no weight here.

"Are you all right, Dr. Wilford?"

I felt tired. And worried. But I maintained my dignity, reminding myself of the reverend's dismissive remarks about the female propensity to emotionality. Recalling this made me angry, and I used this anger to steady myself. Still, I must have given something away as his tone softened in just the way I dreaded it might.

"We seem to have gotten off track here." He reached out a hand and touched my knee. Though a light touch, it was still quite forward. My skin crawled. Sensing as much, he pulled back his hand and continued speaking as if no such action had occurred. "I only mentioned Dr. Ward's initial warnings as a means of reassuring you that, were it not for his thoughtful telephone call, I too might have been blind to Dorothy's essential wickedness. Just as you have been."

I started to speak, but he held up a hand to stop me.

"Please understand," he said. "I don't blame you for what you have or have not perceived. Who can be held to an expectation of perfect knowledge? You received no warning comparable to the one I received from our good doctor. Absent that, it is only human to feel sympathy for a child. Colossians 3:12 says, *'Clothe yourselves with compassion.'* Well, I see that beautiful raiment upon you, Dr. Wilford. And even Dorothy herself is not entirely to blame for sowing the confusion you struggle with. No, it is Satan, who often uses our most sympathetic characteristics to his evil advantage. Your kind heart, for example. The Prince of Lies doesn't make these things easy."

I did not feel taken in by Satan or by Dorothy Gale. I resisted the urge to clarify myself. I hadn't come here so the reverend could become better acquainted with me. I'd hoped to learn something of value from him, but all I had gleaned so far was that his ardor for God was more venomous than I'd feared. I pushed that away and changed the subject. "Was Alvina a regular churchgoer?"

He sighed. "Regretfully, no. Not for many years."

"But at one time she'd been a congregant?"

"As a younger woman."

"You must have been sad to lose her."

"Yes, I tried to bring her back to the flock. I grieve every lost opportunity for salvation."

"Do you believe she's damned?"

"Second Corinthians tells us, *'We must appear before the judgment seat of Christ; that every one may receive the things done in his body, according to that he hath done, whether it be good or bad.'* " He pointed to his desk chair. "This is not the judgment seat of Christ. I can't say what may have befallen Alvina's soul, whatever worries I have about the matter. However, I will say this much. I *wish* Alvina had allowed me to help her cleanse her soul. It saddens me that she didn't. But my ministry goes on. As it must." He removed a watch from his vest pocket, making a display of being surprised by the lateness of the hour. "Speaking of my ministry . . . I should get back to my flock." He made a show of looking about his office. "From the mess in here, you might assume I do no work. I assure you the disarray is the result of my determined focus on the welfare of my parishioners."

"Parishioners like Dorothy Gale."

"Exactly."

"Admirable," I said, trying not to sound ironic.

He waved away my false compliment. Then he extended his hand to help me up from the settee.

I needed no help, but he persisted. So I took his hand and stood.

"Call upon me again, Dr. Wilford, if I can be of service. And may the good Lord keep watch over you."

It was likely just my frame of mind, but his simple blessing seemed somehow threatening. Why should I need to be watched over? "Thank you, Reverend."

He opened the door and politely shook my hand as I took my leave.

The man truly believed Dorothy was diabolical . . .

What's anyone of rational mind to make of that? I have no answer.

I reminded myself of my objective in being here and started for the mayor's office, which is located on the main street in a modest storefront law office behind a plate glass window on which is painted in faux gold letters:

C. Watt-Smith

Attorney-at-law ★For Hire★ Mayor of Sunbonnet

Perhaps I was still recovering my composure from my interview with the reverend. Perhaps I was just weary. Perhaps I needed a moment to think about something else. In any case, I discovered myself standing before the storefront for an unreasonably long time, contemplating the odd arrangement of the words on the glass. Was the phrase "For Hire" actually intended to be suggestive of political graft, interjected as it was between the Honorable Watt-Smith's two current occupations? Lawyer for hire is one thing. But mayor for hire is quite another, almost admirable for its shamelessness. Or was I making too much of improper typography, thereby demonstrating what the Sunbonnet gentlemen I met today would consider my big-city cynicism? Ultimately, I spent little time with the mayor, so I cannot claim to have gained a proper sense of his political trustworthiness.

But there I go, getting ahead of the story.

It remains my intention to record events here as they happened, without offering analytical commentary. Or . . . not too much commentary. I'm ever aware that this scribbling is addressed to you, my dear Professor James—the famous pragmatist who pointed out that "a great many people think they are thinking when they're merely rearranging their prejudices."

CARSON WATT-SMITH

I am tired. My pen hand has grown cramped.

But I will not stop for sleep before sharing with you my meeting with the mayor, who, unlike the other three townsmen, claimed from the moment I entered his office to be too busy for anything but a cursory interview. He'd been informed of my stated business in Sunbonnet and did not indulge any pretense to interest or sympathy with my inquiries. However, it was not his impatience that remains the most powerful first impression of our meeting. As I said before, I have dealt often with contrariness. What weakened my knees and constricted my lungs upon making his acquaintance, what caught me unprepared, was his appearance. Naturally, he knew none of this.

The mayor's gray mustaches and beard are perfectly trimmed, and his slate-gray suit well-tailored. His shirt was as crisp and white as the down of a swan. His cotton cravat was a dignified pale red. His pince-nez framed striking green eyes. In manner he was distinguished as well. He exceeds our East Coast stereotypes of prairie politicians. I understand why

Sunbonnet elected him mayor. But that misses the most significant quality of his appearance, which is that Carson Watt-
Smith bears an unsettling resemblance to a half-dozen old
photographs of my father. When I was a girl of eight, I used to
secretly remove them from deep within my mother's Louis
Vuitton trunk that had travel stickers from the Hôtel Plaza
Athénée in Paris and the Sina Bernini Bristol in Rome. I stud-
ied the photos in hopes of gaining some affinity to the ever-
absent patriarch of our immediate family.

This association distracted me from whatever big-city prejudices I carried with me into the mayor's office. My sensibilities
were rendered brittle by the familiarity of the man's appearance
and the heartbreaking reminder of hearing my late mother talking aloud to those same photographs after she put me to bed and
thought me asleep. The pictures would be three decades old by
now, and so this could not *be* my father, who would be in his
eighties if he is still alive. In that light, you might have expected
me to respond to this stranger with misplaced anger. But instead,
I discovered myself predisposed to *approve* of him. And, worse,
to hope he approved of me! All this in the first moment I entered
the office. Does that make sense, Professor? Oh, my affinity
likely had something to do with the mayor's personality. He's a
politician, after all. (I hope it goes without saying that I was not
attracted to him as a woman is to a man; that is, I was not
charmed in an amorous way; I am not as perverse as that.) But I
knew even as I stepped into his office that I cared what he
thought of me to a degree that exceeded professional boundaries, be it those of psychologist or detective. I suspect this limited
my inquiry. Still, I did not for a moment trust the Honorable
Carson Watt-Smith, not a whit more than I would have trusted
the absent man in my mother's trunk. But enough of that.

You work it out, my dear Professor James.

"I didn't know the Gale girl," Mayor Watt-Smith said, standing with professional bearing beside his desk. He did not offer me a seat. Nor did he seem to note anything unusual in my response to his appearance. I was glad for that. "I don't think I ever met the child. I've little experience of children in general, so frankly, I don't see how I can be of help to your project."

I could have guessed that you've had little experience with children, I thought. But I didn't say it. I knew better than even to hint at the mayor's resemblance to one so near to me—or is it far from me? Watt-Smith would not have understood or sympathized with such a distraction. It would not have softened his bearing toward me. Indeed, such an allusion would have disqualified me from being taken seriously by him. So I gathered myself like a cloak and proceeded as if there was nothing unusual about him. Us. "Perhaps then you can tell me something about Alvina Clough."

"I thought you were researching the Gale girl."

"Yes, but since you don't know her, it could be helpful to learn something about the woman she's accused of assaulting."

"Accused? Accused is just the beginning of it. You've read the transcript of her hearing, I presume."

"I have."

"Then you know the difference between an accusation of guilt and an admission of it."

Once again, I saw no advantage to arguing the point. Besides, it was disorienting hearing the words *accusation* and *admission* coming from his lips, strange because for years I'd imagined such a conversation with one very like him, albeit in a different context.

"What do you want to know about Alvina?" he asked.

"You were her lawyer?"

"Yes."

"Miss Clough's last will and testament."

"I helped her draft the document. What about it?"

That Alvina had updated her will seven years before, changing her beneficiary from the town of Sunbonnet, which her father had founded, to Dorothy Gale had become public knowledge only at the girl's hearing. "Everyone tells me Dorothy had no relationship with Miss Clough. Yet the prosecution asserts that inheritance may have served as a motive to the crime."

"To refer to the 'prosecution' is to misunderstand the nature of the hearing, Dr. Wilford. The state attorneys were not here to *prosecute* the girl. They were here to help her. We provided an official inquiry and spared her a trial for that very reason. Do you understand that?"

Is one who is accused of murder *aided* by being spared a trial and summarily found guilty? "How could Dorothy have known she was beneficiary of the will?"

"I have no idea. Nor did *I* ever assert that she did."

"Who else knew about the inheritance?"

"No one, as far as I know. Perhaps Miss Clough told someone. I can't say. What I *can* say, though, is that I told no one. Sharing details of my clients' business is unethical. Is there anything else? I'm quite busy."

"Do you think it plausible that Miss Clough told someone? Considering her withdrawn personality."

"Possible? Anything is possible."

"I said *plausible.*"

"Oh, that's another thing." He jangled coins in his pockets. "It's extremely unlikely that Miss Clough told anyone about her personal business. She was not naturally forthcoming. And

even if she had mentioned such a thing . . . well, I don't see
how an eleven-year-old farm girl would either have heard
about it or understood the implications."

I gathered my courage. "Why didn't you say as much at
Dorothy's hearing?"

"Why would I have done that?" he asked.

"To counter the accusation that the girl was motivated by
inheritance to commit murder. It's an absurd argument in the
first place. But in light of the unlikelihood of Dorothy's even
knowing about it . . . well, what's the word for something
that's beyond absurdity?"

"Outrageousness," he said.

I looked back to him. "Exactly."

"The assertion of financial motive to Dorothy's crime had
nothing to do with the findings of the hearing." He paused.
The silence stretched. Then he turned around. "The girl confessed, for God's sake."

"To 'melting' a wicked witch," I said. "Not to killing
Alvina Clough."

"You have me wondering, Dr. Wilford. How does all this
apply to your stated purpose here? Your academic research
project about Dorothy Gale, your psychological study. It's
starting to seem like your actual motive among us provincials
may be something else altogether. Have you read one too many
detective stories? Is that it?"

I had no wish to discuss my motives, so I pushed forward.
"Why did Miss Clough leave her money to Dorothy?"

"I don't know."

"You didn't ask her?"

"That wasn't my job. And even if I had asked, I'd be obliged
to keep such an exchange private."

"Even now that Miss Clough is gone?"

"Miss Clough's expectation of privacy does not end with her death. As I said before, my client never told me why she named Dorothy as her benefactor. She was not obliged to do so. And—" Watt-Smith stopped.

"And what?"

"And that's all the time I have for you today, Dr. Wilford."

"Did you know before the reading of the will that Alvina's fortune had dwindled to close to nothing?"

"No."

"But you were her attorney. So—"

He cut over me: "I helped Miss Clough write her last will and testament, but I did not possess power of attorney when it came to her bank account or any other investments she had."

"So the will—"

"Irrelevant, as far as her murder goes. Her finances too are irrelevant, as I see it."

I wished he'd said as much at Dorothy's hearing. It wouldn't have vindicated her, but it couldn't have hurt.

"That really is all the time I have for you today." He moved to his office door and opened it, his expression austere and immobile.

I managed a weak salutation and left his office.

Supper in the hotel dining room, fending off the consecutive advances of cigar-scented salesmen from Missouri and Illinois, occupied the first hour of the evening. Next, a bath, soaking and thinking. Then writing this letter. Hours gone. And now the street outside my hotel room is quiet but for the occasional hooting of an owl or, once, the bloodthirsty shrieks and whoops of coyotes. Some rabbit or opossum has been served up to the pack. Moonlight enters through my window in a startling shade of white. Still, I'm not frightened, even if my interviews indicate that I'm not welcome here. Even if one of the men I spoke to today likely killed a solitary woman in her home and contrived evidence to falsely implicate an eleven-year-old girl.

Or perhaps I *am* terrified but simply don't recognize it. My feelings are blurred now, despite, or perhaps because of, the voluminous recounting of events to which I have subjected you here, my dear professor. Please accept my apologies. I look at the stack of pages scrawled in my hand, and I blush at my use of dialogue and other dramatic techniques that are better suited to your brother Henry's oeuvre than to the objectivity of my training. Or perhaps this stack of words has grown out of the discipline of making contemporaneous notes for psychological cases. Ah, but this is neither a scientific paper nor a case history. I believe more than ever that this is a murder investigation, and so admittedly, my letters to you serve not only as communication with a trusted advisor but also as a means of organizing events so that I might arrive at some useful conclusion. What that conclusion might be I still cannot imagine.

Does that make a failure of all these words? I have discerned no reason why anyone would want to kill Alvina Clough. She seems to have been a cold and antisocial woman. That may have made her unlikeable to many, but wouldn't this same standoffishness actually make her *less* likely a target than, say, a warm and sociable woman whose engagement with others could inspire personal complications? Alvina had to be more than the shrewish loner that townsfolk believed her to be. I feel insufficient clarity to speculate on such a matter. Not at this hour, when all but the lonely or the mad are asleep. I can say with certainty only this much: the writing of this communique has carried me far past any reasonable hour for bed.

"Whistling to keep up courage is no figure of speech." But as I am now too tired to whistle I think it best to turn off my light.

Until tomorrow.

Yours,

Evelyn

P.S. I don't know how many hours have passed since I put down this pen and turned off the light. Tired as I was, I found it impossible to rest. Sleeplessness, my perennial demon. In this instance, it may have served me well, as lying awake I heard footsteps in the hall. Cautious steps that stopped outside my room. I sat up and reached for the gas lamp on the night table, turning it up. Its light must have seeped beneath my door, as the footsteps moved quickly away. After a silent minute or two, I wrapped myself in my coat and cautiously peered into the hall. No one there. But I'll not sleep again tonight. I'll leave the light on and offer the scratching sound of this pen as evidence that I'm still on guard. A murderer does number among the townsfolk on this coyote-haunted plain. Was it him outside my door? It may have been one of the ineffectual out-of-state salesmen drunkenly loitering. That's no pleasant thought either. I do not carry a Derringer in my handbag, but I might, as far as they know. This reassures me. Regardless, I will not be caught unawares.

All will be well.

So, having returned to this poor desk in this otherwise passable hotel room, I will take this opportunity to address something that agitated my mind in the tossing and turning of my sleeplessness. I feel a need to clarify why I have addressed this correspondence to you, Professor James, rather than to a family member or even my fiancé, who is a perfectly intelligent and good-hearted man.

First, allow me to apologize again that your reading of this second letter will have required more than what may cordially be expected of anyone who merely opens an envelope (however thick) and removes what he expects to be an ordinary correspondence. I want you to know, Professor, that I share these notes with you not just as a detailed record of events intended to help me solve a crime. Even less do I offer them to you as justification for my resignation from work as an academic researcher in favor of that of amateur detective. These notes are addressed to you because you are more to me than you may know. More to me than just my trusted mentor. You are my companion, even when you are not here. Please don't misunderstand. I do not mean this in any unseemly romantic sense. I have the utmost respect for the marriage and family that you and Alice share. I know your intentions toward me have never been anything but professional and respectable. When I say you are my companion, I mean that in difficult moments I imagine you being with me, and I ponder on what you might advise, what we might discuss; and thereby I arrive at a more apt course of action. I do not always follow your imagined advice. Would I be here now if that were so? But I also know that I am not alone. Yes, that is it. The important element. Not alone.

In the morning I will talk with Henry and Emily Gale. Except for Henry's drinking at the saloon, they're absent in the life of the town. But they're not absent in the imaginations of the townsfolk, who largely blame the couple for Dorothy's evil ways. An apple doesn't fall far from its tree, etc. Although I cannot claim to be positively inclined toward them—they've never visited their niece in Topeka—I don't subscribe to the town's demonizing theories. I'll hire a wagon to take me to the family farm, a distance of three miles. I'd be lying if I did not acknowledge my trepidation as I consider meeting the pair and standing on the land where Dorothy grew up. Ah, Dorothy . . . I know it's both unprofessional and unwise for me to think of her as my Dorothy, but then it is *also against professional standards to travel to the hometown of a patient to attempt to set matters right. Yet here I am. What is she doing at this moment? Sleeping. I hope she's dreaming of Oz or some other place. Some place kinder than an insane asylum in Topeka, or Sunbonnet, Kansas.*

CHAPTER 14

Regarding the events of September 1896

Sunbonnet, Kansas

Oh, how different it all might have been if the Wilford woman had never come. In the days immediately after Dorothy Gale and the newspapermen left our town, we all enjoyed a collective sense of relief that might have lasted, well, forever. A grateful sense of normality marked the Sunday church service just one week after the train carried the newspapermen away. We believed the town's problems had been permanently resolved. Reverend Richter quoted that day from Psalms 107:29: *"He stilled the storm to a whisper; the waves of the sea were hushed."* The raging storm that had brought to Sunbonnet a powerful and destructive twister was stilled; even more disorienting had been the tempest that brought murder, the sin of Cain, to our own beloved town. That too was stilled; finally, we not only endured but overcame and *set right* the flurry of irreligiosity and evil illness that had characterized the Gale girl and, to a lesser degree, her Aunt Emily and Uncle Henry. In light of this civic fortitude, how could we not share among ourselves a modest and God-fearing sense of well-being? Good seemed to have won out. The order we'd worked all our lives to maintain was restored. We celebrated its return in common decencies shared with one another, be it the tipping of our hats to the good ladies of our town or offers of assistance to any farmer who might require it, particularly as harvest neared. And we were not the only ones to recognize the special providence that characterized our town. In the past three years, Mayor Watt-Smith had overseen electrification, placing Sunbonnet among a mere handful of communities on the prairie to enjoy the brilliance of Edisonian light. He'd also lobbied and convinced the Bell Telephone Company to install a local telephone circuit—a multiparty line. Close to two dozen of their miraculous devices could ring and reach one another here in town by merely cranking a handle. We were not indulging in gratuitous or unwarranted pride. With the Dorothy Gale tragedy behind us, Sunbonnet had been returned to its typical pious state—something worth fighting for. Especially as the very attributes we celebrated also made our town a target of the ever-jealous Devil and his minions. Moral strength and vigilance were our weapons.

Quoting from Proverbs 10:25, the reverend encouraged us thus: *"As the whirlwind passeth, so is the wicked no more, but the righteous is an everlasting foundation."*

However, nothing of this fallen world is truly everlasting.

Close to two months after the Gale girl was sent away, the Wilford woman arrived on a late afternoon train with a suitcase full of store-bought clothing and a head full of dangerous ideas. She hired a handcart to take her luggage from the station to the Peabody Hotel. When she checked in, she paid cash and complimented Patterson the manager on the furnishings of his establishment and the town's friendly atmosphere. She glanced with barely concealed scorn at a handful of harmless but personable salesmen lingering in the lobby. They may have lingered a little longer in her presence than was strictly necessary. The men doffed their hats when she passed on her way upstairs, but their gestures did not soften her demeanor. To all appearances, she was neither an anarchist nor a suffragette. She was a modern woman of the sort with which we hadn't much experience. We gentlemen of Sunbonnet continued for some time to offer her every hospitality. True, this may in part have had to do with her youthful good looks. It's also true that the townswomen of Sunbonnet recognized the more threatening aspect of the Wilford woman before we men did. From the moment she arrived, our wives, sisters, and mothers reminded us that a woman who travels alone is not to be trusted. We gentlemen came soon enough to the same conclusion, even if initially we were taken unawares, victims of our own imperfect human natures.

CHAPTER 15

September 14, 1896

Dear Professor James,

It's now four PM Wednesday, and I am not exaggerating when I say this has been a morning and afternoon of extraordinary significance. The evening ahead promises to be even more consequential. Indeed conclusive. As I've not had time to post either of the previous day's letters, I'm tempted to address this communiqué as merely an additional postscript to last night's overgrown missive. But I reconsidered, fearing that a stylist of such repute as yourself might object to the near-absurdity of a double postscript. Besides, this is a new day, and much of what I wrote previously seems to me now merely prologue. (By tomorrow I will have time and opportunity to post these three letters, though I will have to put them in a box rather than an envelope! Yes, tomorrow, when all will be different.)

The weekly Wednesday night Bible study at the church hall, the next and likely final stop in this affair, is not yet for a few hours, and so I am not as pressed for time as I feel.

So allow me to start at the beginning, my interview with the Gales:

I arrived on their property a few minutes past eight. The farm remains a shambles. The house is nothing but a pile of splintered wood, an emblem of the power of the twister and the inertia that has plagued the Gales since the catastrophe. Still, I suspect I'd have described the place as a shambles even before the storm. Though undamaged by the storm, the barn and corncrib look like they could fall down any moment of their own accord after many years of neglect. I can't imagine this was ever a happy or healthy place for a girl to grow up. When I found Emily and Henry Gale in the barn, I realized it isn't a livable place for adults either.

"Mr. and Mrs. Gale?" I called.

Silence.

The couple has assembled a makeshift residence in one corner of the barn. Borrowed furniture, much of it worthy only of the county dump, is arranged in haphazard fashion on the hard clay floor. A rickety sofa covered with calico. A sagging double bed made up with filthy gingham sheets and pillows. A horsehair chair chewed through by rats. These furnishings stand just ten feet from the stalls of the two dray horses, who observe the scene with their calm and beautiful eyes. Beyond that, three milk cows stand in narrow enclosures, their tails swishing at flies. None of this was initially visible to me; I'd entered from bright sunlight, and the barn was illuminated only by whatever natural light penetrated the open doorway and the narrow gaps between the long, vertical boards that comprise the walls. Any sunlit spaces were marked by hovering dust motes. The rest was in shadow.

"Who are you?" Henry said.

I turned toward the sound of his voice.

"What do you want?" he continued.

I stepped through the big open doorway. The scent of cows, horses, and manure assailed me. "I'd like to speak with Mr. Gale. Are you Mr. Gale?" Moving toward the voice, I closed my eyes in hopes of speeding my adjustment to the dimness. "Mrs. Gale, are you here too?"

"Who are you?" Henry asked again.

I opened my eyes. Now I could see the aged-beyond-their-years couple sitting on straight-back chairs at a square wooden table at one edge of their makeshift accommodations. A coffee pot and two metal cups rested before them. Nothing else. I had heard no sound from within as I approached the barn, and feared I might have to traverse their property to find them. They'd been here all the time, sitting in silence. For how long? Judging from their gray countenances, it could have been centuries. Indeed, the place felt like a kind of purgatory—a place neither here nor there, neither light nor dark. Spectral. My subsequent interaction with Henry and Emily Gale only reinforced this notion.

"My name is Dr. Evelyn Grace Wilford," I said. "I'm a visitor to your town. May I ask a few questions about your niece, Dorothy? I'd like to help her."

Henry gestured to a third chair at the table. "Sit then."

I did as he instructed.

"Nobody comes here no more," he said. A small man dressed in dirty dungarees, Henry's eyes are weary, and his body seems hollowed out. You feel as if you could press on his chest and see your handprint come through on his back. But he is not weak. His mud-caked hands are oversized and solid as stones. "Then again," he continued, "nobody never did come around here. Before the twister neither, I mean. We wasn't never no stop on the social calendar, were we, Emily?"

Emily just glanced away.

She is as gray and wizened as her husband. Her clothing's just as threadbare as Henry's. She wears her hair in a messy bun. When she turned to me, I noted that her eyes focused on a space a few inches above my head. My initial instinct was to look up at whatever she was seeing. But I suspected nothing would be there, so I reached across the table and lightly touched her arm. "Are you all right, Mrs. Gale?"

She shrugged.

"She don't talk no more," Henry said.

I remembered that Dr. Ward had mentioned a seizure.

"Not since the twister," Henry said. "Or leastways not since we learned afterward of the girl's terrible act."

Emily slapped her hands down hard on the table, and I nearly jumped out of my chair.

Henry reached across and grabbed his wife by her right wrist. "She don't like folk talking about what happened with the girl."

Emily turned to him with an angry glare. Once again she stared at a spot a few inches above his head. This time, I looked. Nothing there.

"You gonna be calm?" Henry asked her.

She huffed in answer and pulled her arm away from him.

"She's a strong one," Henry said.

My medical training came to the fore. While it was possible that her mute apoplexy was a psychological manifestation of anguish and upheaval, I agreed with Dr. Ward's appraisal that Emily had suffered an actual episode in her brain. A blood pressure spike followed by the breaking of a blood vessel and subsequent blockage, or some such thing . . . "May I see your hands?" I asked her.

Immediately, she dropped her hands into her lap, hiding them beneath the table.

"Her right hand don't work no more neither," Henry said flatly. "The hand sets kind of funny at the end of her arm, like a dead animal, so she's not too keen to show it."

"She's suffered a stroke, Mr. Gale."

"Yeah."

"Dr. Ward told me he's no longer welcome here."

"What's a doctor gonna do for her now? The thing already happened. Can't be fixed. Sides, I ain't got money to give away to those who don't need it. And you ain't welcome here neither if your only reason for coming is to tell us how to live our lives."

Emily sighed and looked away. Now I understood why she hadn't visited the girl in Topeka or attended Dorothy's legal hearing. My heart went out to the woman. "If I ask you a few questions, can you write out answers?" I asked her.

Henry laughed. "Writing—blah! Em didn't know how to write more than just her name even *before* she lost the use of her hand. She can nod yes or no. So you can go ahead and ask her about the things she can't do no more that are a far sight more important than writing, like can she still boil a pot of water or peel a potato? 'Course, I can answer that for her. *No.* The answer is she can't do *nothing* no more. Look at her. Just a dumb lump of flesh, and if it weren't for me, she'd just sit here and starve to death. So if you want something from us, it'll have to come from me, understand?"

"Your manner with her is reprehensible."

"Repri-what?" he said. "I ain't never heard that word. But if it means that this old woman owes me for keeping her fed and clothed and owes me more than she'll ever be able to repay, then I accept your compliment. Thank you kindly."

"That's not what it means."

"Then you can go straight to hell, miss. You don't know nothing about our lives."

I hated Henry's tone. His bitterness stunk up the barn far more than the horses or cows or manure. But I knew it served no good purpose to storm out without at least asking the questions that had brought me there. Yet I could not speak without betraying my anger and, worse, revealing my damnable sense of powerlessness. I laid my palms flat on the table and took a long breath, as if that were communication enough. Perhaps it was.

"The woman here wasn't going to be able to tell you much anyways," Henry said. He slapped on his broad-brimmed hat. "Come outside into the farmyard, and I'll answer your questions best I can. And then you can be on your way."

I nodded and stepped away from the table, avoiding Emily's off-centered gaze. What would become of her here? Nothing good. But I told myself that what Emily Gale likely wanted most was for me to help her niece, and so I redoubled my determination to do that. "Pleasure meeting you, Mrs. Gale."

She shifted her gaze to a shadowy corner of the barn where Dorothy's small dog, Toto, was curled. Though filthy, his eyes shone. Tied to a post, he cautiously stepped in my direction to the edge of his short leash. He sniffed at the air and then sat down again, as if he had smelled the helplessness I felt. At least he was alive. This alone would cheer Dorothy. I resolved not to leave Sunbonnet without him.

"You coming?" Henry asked.

I followed the farmer back into the blinding sunshine.

He stopped in an empty patch between the barn and the vacant pigpens. "What do you want from us? Can't you see we got nothing left?" He chewed on a quid of tobacco, spitting occasionally onto the dirt. "After the girl done what she done, we can't even get no help no more from the townsfolk—and they was a stingy lot to begin with."

"I didn't come here to make things worse for you."

"Look around you, miss. Take a good long look. You believe for one minute that anything you might do to us could make things worse than they already are?"

I allowed a moment to pass silently, to acknowledge the man's grim predicament, whatever my personal distaste for him. "Mr. Gale, tell me about Dorothy's parents."

"Her kin?"

I nodded.

"I don't know nothing."

He seemed to be toying with me. "She's your niece. Was it her mother or father who was kin to you?"

He waved a hand at a fly buzzing around his face. "Told you. I don't know nothing about it."

"I don't understand."

He spat into the dirt. "The girl weren't actually kin to me."

"What?"

"That's why I thought it best to come outside here to talk, just you and me. Emily don't know none of what I'm telling you. And she's not as addled in her brain as it seems. She can still understand everything she hears, even if she's got no way to answer back. I didn't want to put this afore her, you understand? After keeping it from her for so long. What good would knowing such things do for her now?"

"Knowing what things, Mr. Gale?"

He spat again. "Like I told you, the girl ain't my kin. Nor Emily's."

"But everybody says she is."

"Don't matter what everybody says."

"How did she come to be in your household? And why did you tell everyone she was your niece? Where'd she come from?" With each question my heart beat faster. "What's this about?"

"What's it about? Twenty-seven dollars a month, that's what. Twenty-seven dollars a month is pretty good just to raise a girl who don't eat much." Henry spoke straightforwardly, without shame, as if explaining a day rate for a hired hand or the yield of a milk cow. "It's especially good money when your missus always wanted a child of her own. And kicked and whined about us never having a little one. Pawing off care of the girl on Emily kept her quiet and kept her out of my business. Besides, look around this farm. Do you think we was going to make the mortgage by crops alone? This ain't the best land, and I ain't the best farmer."

"Someone paid you twenty-seven dollars a month to raise Dorothy and claim her as your niece?"

"Yeah."

"Who?"

"Don't know. Never mattered to me. All I know is the money *was* real. Delivered in my name to the train station in an envelope postmarked from St. Louis. Every month on the first. Regular as rain. What did I care who sent it?'

"Who else knew about this?"

"Nobody. If I'd ever told a single soul, then my twenty-seven dollars would have stopped right then. That was spelled out clear to me at the start. But I don't feel the same restriction now. Cause the money's stopped coming anyways. Ever since the girl done what she done. Yeah, it's over for good. I'm in no position to complain. Not leastwise because I don't know who to complain to in the first place. That's why I don't mind spilling it to you. Why the hell not?"

"So, who *is* Dorothy? If she's not a Gale. Where'd she come from an—"

"Don't know. Told you that. Don't care either. What difference does it make? She was a girl who needed a home. Em was a woman who needed a child. And I was a farmer who could make use of twenty-seven dollars a month. Why would I ask questions when everything was going so good for all of us? Even if the girl *was* a pestering aggravation most of the time."

"How did all this come about?"

He looked across the farmyard at the fallow fields. "Got a letter one day."

"From who?"

"Don't know who. It weren't signed."

"What did the letter say?"

"That there was a babe still in swaddling that needed raising. And the twenty-seven dollars a month. And the secrecy." He turned back to me. "That's all."

"How did you get the child?"

"I traveled to Lawrence and picked her up at an address given in the letter."

"Do you remember the address?"

"It was just a house."

"Do you still have the letter?"

"What kind of fool would I be to keep such a thing as that around? Specially since Em was always snooping around my things like she owned the place?"

"And after that?"

"We raised the girl best we could. 'Cause we're Christians."

And because of the twenty-seven dollars a month, I thought. "Did you receive any other letters?"

"Never."

"Nobody ever asked you about Dorothy?"

"In town folks might sometimes say, 'How's the girl?' or sentiments along such lines. Just neighborly. Nothing more than that."

"And what would you say?"

"I'd say, 'She's fine.' What else was there to say? And it weren't untrue neither. Not until she went off and killed that bitter old woman. Then she wasn't fine no more."

"I don't believe she killed Alvina."

"Well, what you believe ain't worth a shovel full of manure." He started back into the barn, holding one hand up in the air as if in farewell. "That's all I got to say to you, miss." Watching him go, I noticed Emily leaning against the big doorway. How long had she been there? Was she close enough to have heard any of what her husband said? And what difference might it make if she had? All I know is that she retreated into the darkness before Henry Gale managed to trudge across the barnyard and reach the barn door.

The muted woman was as broken down as the farm.

But I didn't know how to help her. Not in these circumstances. For all my training, I still don't. Can it be, Professor James, that sometimes there's nothing we can do to help? Yet Henry has effectively buried the poor woman in his junk pile. From what Dorothy told me in Topeka, her aunt always treated her with kindness. Doubtless, Emily is grieving for her loss. I

wished I could console her. But then I suspected and still believe
now that my going back inside that dark place would only have
resulted in further cruelty directed to Emily from her husband.
I'd only make matters worse. So, helpless and frustrated, I
headed down the road toward my hired wagon and driver. And
on that brief walk, my thoughts proceeded from Emily's predicament to what Henry had told me about his "niece," and I
wondered:

Who is Dorothy Gale?

Who sent twenty-seven dollars every month?

"Didn't I warn you, miss?" The skinny young man from the
livery helped me onto the dusty buckboard. "See what I meant,
miss?" He settled himself behind the team and took up the
reins. "That farm isn't just blighted. It's cursed. It'd have to be,
considering what the girl who grew up there did to that old
woman. Can't say I didn't warn you, miss. The whole way
here."

He'd talked the entire trip, telling me nothing I didn't
already know.

"I watched you walk up to the wagon just now. And since
I'm the observant type, I could see you'd been upset by whatever happened over there with the old Gale fella. Didn't I say
you'd find nothing worthwhile at that farm? Should have listened to me. Nothing worthwhile."

The boy was right. I'd been upset. But my time with the
Gales *had* been worthwhile. And sad too. But an experience
needn't be just one thing. Talking with Henry had inspired a
new line of inquiry about Dorothy, even as it left me feeling
helpless when it came to Emily. I wasn't going to explain any
of this to the glib livery boy. I owed him nothing—except the

two bits I'd agreed to pay for transport from town and back. "Please may we just go?"

He shook the reins, we started back, and he dropped me at the hotel.

I intended to go to my room to freshen myself from the stench of the shadowy barn and the general squalor of the broken-down farm. And that wasn't all I hoped to cleanse away. Talking with Henry had left me feeling truly soiled. Perhaps a more intrepid detective would not have felt the need for a bath at this time. But frankly, I didn't know what my next step should be anyway. I needed time to think, to soak. I questioned if running about Sunbonnet asking townsfolk for commentary about Dorothy and Alvina was a productive investigative approach. The front desk man handed me my key without his usual greeting. I was grateful for the brief exchange and even more so that the lobby at midday was empty of strutting, big-bellied salesmen trying out their personal pitches on me. I walked up the stairs. But as I put my key in the door to my room, and entered . . .

It turned out this was no time for a bath, after all.

First, I nearly stepped on an envelope that had been slipped under my door. A correspondence from management? I picked it up. There was nothing written on the front, so I slipped my finger under the glued flap. However, before opening it, I noticed that my suitcase on the stool at the foot of the bed wasn't in the same position as I'd left it. Who'd been here? As there was no housekeeping service at this hotel, no one had good reason to enter my room. I tossed the envelope on the desk next to this stack of pages. I then went to the suitcase, in fear I had been robbed. Although nothing was missing, someone had rifled through its contents, and my personal items had been put back in an untidy fashion. I glanced about the room for any further sign of interference with my things. Nothing else looked out of order. My heavy coat and dresses hung just as I had left them in the bureau. Still, I felt a chill at the thought of someone having been in here, rummaging. Who? Why? The invasion reminded me that my visit here is no mere academic inquiry. The stakes are high. Then I glanced to the desk, at the stacked pages that comprised my two unmailed letters to you. Had the intruder read them? I couldn't recall exactly how I had left the stacks arranged on the desk and couldn't tell if they had been perused. But I considered everything I shared with you . . . everything I was thinking . . . Someone *had* been in this room. And while it may only have been the desk clerk acting on some perverse invasion of my privacy, wouldn't that be enough to elicit a quickening heartbeat for a woman traveling alone? And if it was something more sinister than that? I thought of the footsteps in the hall last night . . . But what could I do besides wedging a chair beneath the doorknob to deter anyone from returning while I was here?

Only after that did I pick up the envelope.

Inside were five torn pieces of a single page of stationery and one piece of hard candy. The towheaded boy from the sheriff's office . . . Todd, my sweet-toothed partner in crime, the closest thing I have to a friend in this town. A note from him written on scraps? Todd can't write. He can't read either. But with the candy he identified himself as having delivered the envelope. I arranged the five torn pieces on the desktop, fitting them together like a puzzle. It wasn't difficult. They formed the bottom two-thirds of a page of good-quality personal stationery. I looked in the envelope again. Nothing else. The top third of the page was missing. What was left was tightly packed with tiny, finely hand-printed words:

All these years . . . But God knows that doesn't change the fact that the girl is our daughter. Neither the fallen nature of Man nor the plain foolishness of a summer twelve years ago excuses our transgression. Oh, we've seen to our responsibilities so far as Dorothy's care and feeding, but that doesn't mean I would hesitate even at this late date to tell the truth to the world. I have no reputation to soil. But you do. So understand this. The same blood that ran through that girl's veins ran through my blessed father's veins and I will not have Clough blood drying like caked mud in a ditch! Her body will not be defiled by the birds and other wretched vermin that live on this prairie. Tornados happen. Girls are swept up and die. Nothing to be done. But after sustaining the girl's life through this charade for all these years I will not have her death weigh now as an anchor on my conscience. She will be found and given a proper Christian burial, and only then will our responsibility be complete. I know there was an effort today to find the body. But it was feeble. Ten men? This is a big land. Engage every townsperson if necessary. Let them leave the hammering, sawing, piling of broken wood, and repairs. Just find the body. You are a very important man in this town and can make it happen. You will make it happen. Consider yourself advised. You have forty-eight hours. After that, the girl's body will be defiled beyond decency. Forty-eight hours. Then I swear I'll share the truth with townsfolk. Our sin. Our daughter. Why not? They hate me already. What will you say then? What will you do?

*In lieu of a decent Christian burial for the girl, my public
confession will serve as atonement. You may still save yourself. But the clock is ticking.*

A.

*p.s. The winds last night pulled a shutter loose on my porch
and the thing shattered my front window. I will appreciate your
sending a glazier post haste. The mess is unbearable to me.*

I read the note twice. The second time as breathlessly as the
first. Alvina was Dorothy's mother?

I wrestled with the notion. The wretched old woman? The
recluse? The witch?

But Alvina wasn't as old as her manner of living and wilted
reputation made her seem. She'd only have been around forty
at the time of Dorothy's birth. Entirely possible. Still, in a town
as small as Sunbonnet, how could such a thing be kept secret?
And as you likely already figured, Professor James, the woman's yearlong absence coincided with the period she'd have
been with child, in her confinement. A tour of European capitals? Isn't it more likely that she journeyed only as far as a home
for such circumstances in St. Louis or Indianapolis or Chicago?
For better or worse, that's how such things work.

Mightn't Alvina have obtained the souvenirs she passed
around to important townsfolk simply by writing away for
them from overseas during her time away? Given a year, such
trinkets are easily enough obtained from anywhere. Besides,
didn't townsfolk describe her gifts as an uncharacteristic display of generosity? And yet such largesse make sense when
viewed as a ruse, a diversion from Alvina's actual location during that year, her actual condition.

And, more importantly, doesn't this explain why Dorothy Gale was named as the woman's beneficiary? What it all amounted to was this: Dorothy was Alvina's daughter. *Is* her daughter. My inclination to disbelief dissolved. Nothing else makes sense. Besides, here were the woman's words written in what had to be her own hand!

I suspect, Professor, that you have read into the paragraph above something or other about *me*. Having trained under you, I know you will be temperamentally and professionally unable to divorce what I've just written from the circumstances under which you and I met; that is, when I was having personal difficulties after my own experience of just such a home for wayward women. I cannot allow myself to stop and indulge any of that just now. The parallels are thin. I did not anonymously pawn off *my* child on a disinterested and struggling dirt farmer and his sincere but woebegone wife while secretly observing the girl's childhood from a safe and shuttered existence nearby. As you well know, the family to which my girl was delivered is both loving and financially secure, and I've never since darkened the child's joyful existence by casting a prying shadow over her. Surely you appreciate that difference.

Nor did I shutter myself away afterward. No, I drew inspiration from your assistance and came to be your student and then a practitioner of helping others. I hope you don't believe that my presence here in Sunbonnet plays some part in an effort to atone for mistakes. I'm not providing care for another woman's child in place of the maternal care I cannot offer my own . . .

This is precisely the sort of thing I do not have time to consider now. May I remind you that a murder has occurred, and an innocent girl has been incarcerated? That is no mere invention. No psychological construct. Alvina's letter revealed far more than just the identity of Dorothy's mother and the perverse means by which she sought to both support and observe her daughter while remaining anonymous. The letter also revealed that Dorothy's father likely committed the heinous crime and purposefully implicated his own daughter in his place! Please set aside your psychologist's perspective and allow me to carry on with my work here. It may not be the work for which I've been trained but is nonetheless the most important I've ever undertaken.

So, the unknown recipient of the letter was Dorothy's father. *Is* her father.

But who is he?

This much is clear: he's an important man in this town. This rules out Henry Gale. But it doesn't contradict my suspicion that Alvina's killer must be one of the four men who knew about Dorothy's claim to have melted a witch before anyone else. The quadrumvirate are all influential figures around here. Doctor, sheriff, minister, mayor. Additionally, the letter provides a motive for the crime: Alvina's threat to betray her secret, *their* secret, to the town. But to which of the four men was the letter addressed? I quickly catalogued their features, wondering if eye or hair color or the set of the nose or lips might indicate a resemblance between father and daughter. This only led me in mental circles. None of the men resembled her. All of them resembled her. Even if I could point to a facial similarity, it would *prove* nothing. Had one or another said something during my interviews yesterday that might have betrayed his identity? I picked up my pile of pages that precede this one and read through what I'd recorded last night. Nothing incriminating presented itself. Then I realized what must have been obvious to you long ago, Professor James.

I thought of Todd.

He had slipped the missive beneath my door. I could simply ask him from which office he'd gotten it. As you can imagine, my mind raced. The boy must have saved the scraps since the week of the crime. That's a long time. But as he doesn't know how to read, how had he recognized them as important in the first place? Had he shown the reconstructed section of letter to anyone else? Standing in this room little more than an hour ago, I realized there was no reason to torment myself with these questions. Not when I could go and ask Todd himself. So I pulled the wedged chair away from the door, stepped into the hallway, and locked my door behind me (for whatever good that does). Then I headed down the stairs.

I rang the bell at the front desk.

Patterson, the manager, emerged from the back. "Yes?"

"Did you go into my room while I was out this morning?"

An expression of shock. "Absolutely not, miss."

"Did you see anyone come into this hotel during those hours?"

"No. The business gentlemen left early with their wares and have not yet returned."

"No one?"

"I may have been in the back going over the books . . ." Patterson said.

Useless, I thought. But it needn't matter. I had a better lead to follow. So I rushed out of the hotel to find the boy. I found him in the alley beside the mayor's office. He sat alone on a step, polishing a pair of men's shoes.

"Todd?"

"Hello, miss."

"Did you slip that envelope under my hotel room door, Todd?"

". . . Yes."

"Can you tell me where you got it? It's very important."

"Did you eat the candy?"

"Not yet, thank you. Where'd it come from, can you remember?"

"The candy?"

"No. The letter."

"Don't know."

"What do you mean? You must know where you got it."

"From one of the offices I clean."

"Which one? "

"I don't know."

"How can you not know?"

". . ."

"I'm sorry, Todd. I don't mean to be short with you. I just don't understand."

"When I clean the offices, I put all the paper trash into one big sack. And sometimes when I'm done, I sort through it before I dump it all in the fire at the black-smith's. I've found pennies before. That's how I found that torn-up letter, sorting through the whole heap of it afterwards by myself. So I don't know which office it came from."

"When did you find it?"

"I don't recall the exact day, but it was right after the twister. I remember that because everybody's office was so dusty it took twice as long to do my work."

"And you didn't find any other pieces of the torn-up letter?"

"No. But I put together the pieces I had. Just to see if I
    could. Like a puzzle."

"I did the same thing."

"It's a pretty easy puzzle."

"Todd, can you read?"

"Yes."

"Oh, I thought . . ."

"Well, a few words."

"Did you read what was written on that paper?"

"Not exactly."

"What do you mean?"

"I saw a word I recognized."

"What word?"

"*Dorothy.* It was written on the torn-up page in the middle
    of all the other words."

"You picked out that one word?"

"Didn't I tell you she taught me how to write her name? I
    can read it when I see it."

"And that's why you saved that torn page all this time?"

"Yes."

"Just because you saw her name written on it?"

"Well, I like Dorothy. Even though everyone else doesn't.
    But since she's never coming back, I figured I'd share
    the paper scraps with you, because I think you like her
    too."

"I like her very much. Did you show this note to anyone else?"

"No. What's it say? The other words that aren't *Dorothy*?"

". . . Not too much."

"Nothing?"

"No, not nothing."

"So, what?"

"It just says that Dorothy likes you too."

"That can't be, miss. I didn't see my name written in it. I'd have known that. T-O-D-D. Telegraph pole, circle, and two half circles pointing to the right. That's how my name goes. I looked for it."

"Well, it doesn't have your name, but it does say she likes a fair-haired boy. That's you."

"I guess it could be."

"I think so, Todd. I've one more question—as important as the last."

"Okay."

"If somebody breaks their window in Sunbonnet, who would they go to for help replacing it?"

"If they broke the glass?"

"Yes."

"I didn't break nobody's window."

"I'm not saying you did. I'm just asking, Who would you go to?"

"Mr. Garrison does that. I've seen him sometimes with a big glass pane strapped to his back. He's the one."

"Mr. Garrison? Runs the dry good store?"

"Yeah."

"Thank you, Todd. Goodbye for now."

I left Todd to his boot-blacking and headed to the general store. On the way, it occurred to me that the Alvina's postscript could be a clue to the identity of the letter's recipient. I didn't need to know the particular office in which Todd had found it or the salutation to identify the recipient. All I needed to know was who had asked Mr. Garrison, the storekeeper and glazier, to repair the broken window in Alvina's house.

It didn't work out as I'd hoped.

"Miss Clough's broken window?" Mr. Garrison said. "Sure. I done it. Big window too."

I stood at the counter near the cash register. The store was otherwise unoccupied. "Who asked you to fix it?"

He was a rotund man, and when he narrowed his eyes in concentration, they almost vanished within the puffed folds of his face. He set his hand on the shelf where tobacco products were displayed. "Can't recall the name. Distinguished sort of fella."

"It was no one you knew? No one from town?"

"Somebody from a bank in Lawrence, come to claim the house for Alvina's creditors."

"Bank? When was this?"

"Don't know. I could look in my receipt book. Have you got a minute?"

"I don't need the exact day. Just roughly when he asked you to fix the window."

"Few weeks after Alvina died. Maybe a month."

"No one asked you earlier?"

"Earlier?"

"The week the Gale girl went missing?"

"Week of the twister? No. Nobody."

"So, the window was left broken all that time?"

"Yeah. Why?"

"Nothing," I said. And nothing is what I accomplished.

I wandered the main street for a half hour before making my way back to the hotel. I suddenly realized that nothing I'd learned of Alvina suggested she'd have waited for an hour or two for Mr. Garrison to repair her window. Wasn't she both fastidious and demanding? Why had she neither complained nor pursued repairs on her own in the days after she delivered the letter? One possibility came to mind. Had she been killed shortly after delivering the letter rather than two nights later? Someone might have poisoned or smothered her or used some other vicious means that didn't leave wounds or signs. And then, two days later, after hearing about Dorothy's homicidal claim of "melting a witch," someone quickly returned to the scene to desecrate the undiscovered body in a manner calculated to implicate the girl. Two steps, not one. The timeline was possible. Even likely.

But what of it?

True, I'd uncovered a twelve-year-old story of illicit relations between Alvina and one of the town's most respectable principals. I'd come to understand Dorothy's secret birth and the twenty-seven dollars per month child-rearing arrangement. Finally, the letter specified a motive for the murder. But I didn't come here to identify scandal or to further complicate the details of what was always an unsettled case. No, I'd come to gain freedom for Dorothy Gale by identifying the actual killer. I was no closer to that than I'd been when I first stepped off the train in Sunbonnet, as I had suspected that one of the quadrumvirate had to be guilty. So I paced my room, frustrated and fearful of what my failing could mean to the sweet girl in the asylum. I confess I almost gave up. At last, I collapsed in the big chair beside the window and, exhausted, must have fallen asleep for a few minutes; in that time, I dreamed I was back in the big common room of the Topeka Insane Asylum, interviewing Dorothy:

"I've let you down."
"No, Dr. Evelyn Grace Wilford. You're simply not finished yet."

"I don't know what to do next. It makes me *feel* finished."

"We measure ourselves by many standards. Our strength and our intelligence, our wealth, and even our good luck, warm our hearts and make us feel ourselves a match for life. But deeper than all such things, and able to suffice unto itself without them, is the sense of the amount of effort we can put forth."

At this, I awoke. The dream seemed real, but I immediately realized that Dorothy's words of encouragement were not hers, but yours, Professor James. I recalled the exact passage from your *Principles of Psychology*. As long as I have effort to put forth, I'm not beaten. Is that what Dorothy meant in the dream? Is that what you meant when you wrote the words? But wasn't I already putting forth my best effort? Hadn't I spent hours in Topeka analyzing the transcripts of Dorothy's hearing and studying telephone records? And then traveling here, talking to unwelcoming men? And the sleeplessness of last night as I spent the whole of the silent hours writing to you in hopes that by doing so I might break through to an insight that has not come? Effort, yes. Perhaps I'm being called upon to make a different kind of effort, to set aside not only my creeping sense of inadequacy but also my drive toward analysis and to allow myself instead simply to "notice or attend to the present moment of time," as you suggest elsewhere in your book.

I had little choice but to do just that.

I resisted pacing the room, window to wall and back again, and sat on the end of the bed, breathing steadily and releasing the compulsion to understand, analyze, or solve anything. My effort was simply to attend to the present moment of time. An effort at no effort, as you sometimes advise. And then, a question interrupted my calm: Might it be that I already know all I need to know *in this moment*, even if I cannot yet name the killer? Could it be that I am precisely where I need to be? Then a new idea delivered itself to me like a telegram from the deepest ether.

If not the answer to my essential question, it could be the means by which I could discover it.

There was a simple test to which I could put the quadrumvirate to determine which of the four is Dorothy's father and hence Alvina's murderer. A test less complex than those we administered to volunteers in your laboratory, Professor James, but equally elegant. And what better place to administer such a test than at tonight's Bible study, which Dr. Ward asserted is regularly attended by all the best people of Sunbonnet? I don't need all the best people to be there (except as witnesses).

I only need the four.

Renewed, encouraged, and with close to two hours to occupy before leaving my room for the church hall, I moved to the desk and picked up my pen to bring my missive up to the moment—up to *this* moment. And so here we are. I could provide more detail about my proposed experiment. I could describe the protocol easily enough. But I prefer to put my test into practice and report its results to you afterward. So, absent any illusion that I have completed this correspondence, I will note here only that it is time for me to take my coat from the peg on the wall, place my hat properly upon my head, and depart this hotel for whatever awaits among Reverend Richter's congregation. Oh, and one last thing: I must empty the bowl of apples on the end table into my bag to take with me.

More to come, dear Professor . . .

CHAPTER 16

Regarding Events of the Evening of September 14, 1896

Sunbonnet, Kansas

We townsfolk made our ways to the church hall for the Wednesday night meeting, anticipating that Reverend Richter would begin as usual with a reading from Scripture and thereafter would invite a volunteer among us to go up to the lectern to say a few words about what the passage meant to him or her. Yes, our town's good women often share their impressions with the congregation. We accept the teachings in 1 Timothy 2:12 *"Do not suffer a woman to teach, nor to usurp authority over the man, but to be in silence."* But we also believe that women should be encouraged at appropriate times to share their inspiring emotional reactions to the Lord's good news, just as children need be encouraged to express their joy in a Christmas pageant. Then, after the congregant's comments, we expected the reverend would return to the lectern and invite further discussion, which he always directed skillfully. He never made vain show of his considerable learning, but still managed to assuage any ambiguity in the moral teachings of the evening's passage. These are fine, well-attended meetings. Whatever brief socializing occurs afterward is frosting on the cake. Then it's back to our modest, well-kept homes for a night's sleep, which, despite the challenges of daily life on this blessed but unforgiving prairie, is almost always peaceful. We understand our place in the Lord's good plan. But on this Wednesday it didn't come to pass in this way. And blood was spilt as a result.

Are we blameless? No.

It is true that as we entered the church hall, Dr. Evelyn Grace Wilford's unexpected arrival in our town two days before was still a topic of hushed conversation. No sense denying it. But no one thought she would be at the meeting. Nor less that she would alter it. None imagined she could. Short of Sunday services, this was our community's most solemn gathering. So when we noticed with surprise that she was in attendance, seated by herself in the front row, with a large handbag held on her lap, our response was little more than a few quickened whispers and raised eyebrows, but no alarm. The more credulous among us even speculated that her presence meant she was a believer and, in this way, one of us, however self-important and secular her city ways seemed. The credulity was ill placed. If there is one thing that can be said now with certainty about the violent and chaotic events of that night, it is that Dr. Wilford was never one of us.

Reverend Richter took his place at the lectern, the room grew quiet, and the meeting began much as usual. Ever dignified, he offered a warm welcome to all and made special mention of Dr. Wilford, referring to her as our out-of-town guest. She smiled and nodded, but at the same time she pulled her bag closer to herself, as if feeling somehow threatened by the warmth we offered her. Our neighborliness toward her may seem foolish now, but it had been at such a meeting as this only a few weeks before that we had discussed Hebrews 13, taking special note of the beautiful admonition to *"be not forgetful to entertain strangers: for thereby some have entertained angels unawares."* Some among us even responded to Reverend Richter's special welcome to Dr. Wilford with modest applause.

"As always, my heart is warmed to see such a fine gathering here tonight," the reverend said. "You all look ruddy cheeked and it's evident the Lord's blessing is upon our community. How good it is to be here together, not only to give thanks but also to draw more deeply and meaningfully into our hearts and minds the Lord's word. Tonight's passage is from the Book of Matthew, chapter 10. For those with Bibles, please open them now."

We opened our Bibles quickly, leaving time enough to glance at Dr. Wilford.

As some of us suspected, she had brought no Bible to the meeting. And worse, when Carson Whitfield, who sat a row behind her and always came to meetings with a spare Bible tried to give her his, she declined. And indicated with a nod of her head that she would rather focus her attention on Reverend Richter's reading at the lectern. Though she offered Whitfield a friendly enough smile, it still struck us as discourteous.

The reverend cleared his throat and commenced reading:

Fear not them who kill the body, but are not able to kill the soul: but rather fear him who is able to destroy both soul and body in Hell. Are not two sparrows sold for a farthing? And yet one of them shall not fall on the ground dead without your Father knowing. The very hairs of your head are all

*numbered. Fear ye not therefore, ye are of more value than
many sparrows.*

We nodded our heads in response to the comforting words.
Yes, Satan was to be feared. But since much of the Bible spells
out ways the Evil One can be resisted, such fear is manageable.
Even more reassuringly, death needn't be feared at all. A devout
life renders death but a passage in accordance with God's plan.
The reverend would reveal additional layers of depth and
meaning when he elaborated on the passage. But first, as was
his custom, he called for a volunteer to briefly replace him at
the lectern. A volunteer willing to share his or her personal
response to the Lord's good news.

Without hesitation, Dr. Wilford responded by standing.
"May I?" she asked the reverend before facing the rest of us.
"Would you kind folks mind if I spoke my peace?"

What could any of us or the reverend say?

"Please, Dr. Wilford."

We sat up a little straighter as she moved to the front.

"Thank you," she said, setting her big handbag on the floor
beside the lectern.

Reverend Richter moved a few feet to one side.

Dr. Wilford is not a large woman; neither is she graced by
sufficient years to possess the seriousness that some ladies gain
after decades of motherhood and travail. Rather, she's slight
and still of child-bearing age. Although she is nearing thirty
and unmarried and approaching spinsterhood, yet she com-
manded our full attention. The atmosphere grew charged,
almost as if Nikola Tesla had released his hair-raising electricity
into the room. Maybe it was the novelty of her presence. She
was an exotic bird among us country sparrows. Or maybe it

was her ties to the murderous Gale girl, an association that threatened the peace of mind we'd fought to regain when we'd lost our better selves during the legal hearing two months before.

"It's been my pleasure these past days to make the acquaintance of your fine town," she began.

"I was particularly privileged yesterday to spend time with four of your finest citizens: Dr. Ward, Sheriff Hutchins, Reverend Richter, and Mayor Watt-Smith. "I wonder if I may ask these four gentlemen to join me here at the lectern and to stand beside me, as I am not at ease with public speaking. Please come up, so I may share with all of you my deepest held feelings and convictions. Gentlemen?"

For a moment, no one moved. But then Reverend Richter stepped closer to her and said, "This is unusual, Dr. Wilford. But we are a close community, so we're all here to support one another."

Dr. Ward, Sheriff Hutchins, and Mayor Watt-Smith each looked surprised but sufficiently generous of spirit. They shuffled along their rows to the aisle and joined the reverend and Dr. Wilford at the front.

Dr. Wilford waited silently.

The men stood two on each side. Dr. Wilford nodded to each and then returned her attention to us, the audience.

"I believe it's written in the Gospels that the truth shall set you free," the woman said.

We looked at one another.

★　★　★

Should we have immediately recognized what seems obvious now? Turning our community's weekly Bible discussion to any other purpose than increasing our knowledge of the Lord's words is an act of blasphemy, bound to result in the suffering that accompanies any turning away from the Lord. It's easy to see that now, but we were disarmed and manipulated by Dr. Wilford's devious use of the famous quote from John 8:32. Besides, what were we to say? Who would speak out against truth setting you free? And so we allowed what ought to have been stopped in its tracks to proceed past the danger point.

"I have in my possession a letter written by your long-time neighbor Alvina Clough in the last days of her life." The doctor reached into her big handbag and removed an envelope. She withdrew a few torn pieces of writing paper and placed them on the lectern, taking a moment to fit them together. "This letter, while incomplete, reveals not only the true motive of the woman's murder . . ."

A collective gasp rose from the crowd.

Dr. Wilford did not hesitate. "It also reveals, in a subtle way, the identity of the killer—who was *not* Dorothy Gale."

Some among us stood, unable to contain our agitated curiosity.

Others objected, including three of the four men standing onstage around Dr. Wilford.

"What is this?" Mayor Watt-Smith moved to Dr. Wilford's side to see the paper on the lectern.

"This is beyond inappropriate," announced Dr. Ward.

Reverend Richter agreed. "We are having a discussion of the Lord's good word, Dr. Wilford. This is not a carnival side show."

Dr. Wilford remained steadfast, her hands gripping the lectern. The violence to come might have been averted if the objections of our mayor, our doctor, and our reverend had been heeded. The woman's words piqued the interest of many, but this first of two opportunities to turn back the bloody tide was lost when Sheriff Hutchins held up a hand to still the assembly, and surprised us. In a voice that belied his neat and well-mannered appearance, he called out:

"Give the woman a chance to speak."

The three other men gawped at him in surprise. After a moment of confusion, they stepped back.

"Thank you, Sheriff," the lady doctor said.

Sheriff Hutchins pointed a finger in admonition. "Only a moment."

"I'll be brief."

It remains a mystery to us what the sheriff was thinking by letting her go on. Afterward, he failed to provide any good answers. We can't say if he's come up with an answer even now; as he was rightfully discharged within days of the terrible events that followed the Wilford woman's visit to the weekly Bible meeting. What possessed others of our town elders to remain compliant in those first moments is likewise inscrutable. Perhaps the sheer unexpectedness of the Wilford woman's outrageous assertions. Or was it residual interest in the crime? Or weakness of another kind, as Dr. Wilford Presented an attractive female form? Speculation is useless. Better to simply relate events as they occurred.

"Twelve years ago, Alvina Clough left Sunbonnet for a year," the Wilford woman began. "Many of you remember this. But she didn't leave to tour the capitals of Europe, as she told you, but to give birth in secret to a child who was conceived here—conceived by Alvina and one of your own."

"This is downright slanderous," the mayor said.

"What's the fool woman doing?" Dr. Ward asked sharply.

The Reverend glanced daggers at the woman. "What impiety is this?"

"Impiety?" Dr. Wilford said. "But this has everything to do with the fall of a sparrow, as in Matthew."

"How dare you speak of the Gospels this way?" the reverend said.

"You're out of order, miss," the mayor said.

It would have been put to a stop right then if the sheriff had not again intervened. "Let her speak," he barked. His tone took us by surprise, as Sheriff Hutchins ordinarily displayed a mild manner.

"Her intentions are dissolute," the reverend observed.

"I said, let . . . her . . . speak," the sheriff repeated. Foolish, foolish man.

We take pride in being a law-abiding community. In this instance, we were too respectful of a man with a star.
"The child of this secret union is Dorothy Gale."

Watching Moses part the Red Sea could not have so thoroughly stunned us.

"And who is the father?" she asked. "The answer to this question is important not only because it will reveal Dorothy's parentage, but because it also reveals the identity of Alvina's killer. Yes, they are one and the same. The father. The murderer. Allow me now to read what remains of Alvina's letter, written in her own hand on the day after the twister."

The four men looked over her shoulder at the pieced-together paper as Dr. Wilford read the letter. Mayor Watt-Smith and Dr. Ward nodded as if recognizing the writing.

As for us . . . why did we listen to such profane rumor? Sunbonnet is but a small town on the vast and cruel prairie; it is no heavenly vale. Nor are we angels. Our values are stronger than most, but we remain here among the fallen for good reason. Yes, we share in guilt for the catastrophe that followed. We could have left the church hall as a body, refusing to engage with scandalmongering. Yet self-recrimination can be taken too far. If our town is no heavenly vale, neither is it Sodom and Gomorrah. It was not prurience alone that motivated us. It was this too: we are a trusting people. We recalled the reference to John 8:32 with which Dr. Wilford began her talk—innocently believing she was here as a servant to the truth.

The letter. A veritable catechism of blasphemy:

An illegitimate birth; an anonymous arrangement with Henry Gale to raise the bastard child as his orphaned niece in exchange for a monthly remittance. Then there's the girl's disappearance during the twister, the threatening letter from Alvina to the still-unnamed father, who panicked and murdered her. Then Dorothy's unexpected return to Sunbonnet and her odd claim to have "melted a witch." The murderer's opportunistic return to Alvina's house and desecration of her body to implicate the innocent girl. And finally, the logic of reducing the number of suspects to the four men standing now beside Dr. Wilford.

Hurried and only vaguely sensible, it was a malicious interpretation of unrelated events. Was *any* of it real? Still, we had listened, compelled as if by dark, supernatural powers.

Meantime, word must have spread through town that something of unusual interest was happening in the church hall. As the best of us were there already, we can only speculate how news of the Wilford woman's intrusion was passed among the local farmhands, the self-involved, and the morally derelict. It must have been an enthusiastic description because many of these townsfolk rarely attended Sunday services. They pressed into the crowded hall. Among them was Henry Gale, who had come from the saloon, the only place in town he ever showed his face anymore. At first we didn't notice him standing among the others as our attention remained on the group at the stage. Perhaps if we'd noticed him, we'd have taken precautions.

"I have a means to determine who Dorothy's father is." Dr. Wilford opened her bag and brought out five apples that she set before her on the lectern. Four red and one green. Ought we to have taken warning from the symbolic meaning of the apple as it relates to the temptation of Eve in the Garden of Eden? That's an observation made easily enough with the luxury of time and distance. But in that moment the apples were only fruit. "Dorothy Gale suffers from color blindness," Dr. Wilford continued. "She cannot distinguish between shades of red and green. This characteristic was noted first by her schoolteacher and then by Dr. Ward. In medicine, we've learned that color blindness does not develop because of illness or injury, but is an inherited trait, passed from father to child. Yes, father to child." She returned the apples to her big bag and turned to the four men standing around her. "I will ask each of you, in turn, to look inside the bag and choose the green one. Simple."

Reverend Richter pushed past the others and shouldered Dr. Wilford out of the way to reclaim his place at the lectern. He spoke with biblical fury. "This is a travesty. We've come here tonight to discuss the word of the Lord. This is no music hall. Nor court room. This blasphemy must stop now."

"There's no need for a test," the sheriff said soberly.

The Wilford woman started to speak.

The sheriff held up his hand to stop her. "There's no need because we already know."

Indeed we did.

Reverend Richter's inability to tell red from green was a yearly source of holiday merriment when he helps the Ladies Auxiliary decorate the church hall for the Christmas pageant. But we did not doubt his innocence. No, we sat up straighter to watch him dismantle the woman's vicious implications. How would our cherished reverend, so powerful in the pulpit, put the damnable woman in her place?

As we waited, Henry Gale stepped rapidly through the crowd, stinking of liquor, and made a straight line for the stage, where he withdrew from his coat his Remington .44 revolver. He held it before him as if he were back with Quantrill's Raiders aligned on Willow Creek in the Battle of Baxter Springs. He fired at the reverend. His aim was true. The reverend flew backward from the lectern as the gunshot rang out in the hall. A ghastly shriek arose from the ladies, and some of us ducked into the aisles between the chairs while others made for the exits. It all happened so fast. It all happened so slowly. And then the second shot. At first we didn't know where it had come from. But we saw Henry Gale wilt to his knees and fall backward, a bullet hole in the center of his forehead. That's when we noticed the pistol in the sheriff's hand, taken from the holster he wore beneath his unassuming suit coat.

An unsettling silence settled over the hall. Shock. But not for long. As if on cue, more shrieking and shouting arose.

Mrs. Richter ran to the front of the hall, where her husband lay dying.

★　★　★

Mrs. Richter knelt beside her husband, saying words we did not at first understand. Townsfolk who remained in the hall, which smelled now of discharged gunpowder, watched mutely.

Dr. Ward ripped open Henry's blood-soaked shirt only to discover there was nothing to be done. Beside him, the sheriff stood ramrod straight, taking deep, rapid breaths in an attempt to regain his composure. At the sheriff's side, the mayor stared at the ceiling, unwilling to observe the scene at his feet. The Wilford woman stood wide-eyed, with her arms crossed, her hands gripping each opposite shoulder. Her bag had been tipped during the melee, so apples lay now around the dying man. Four red and one green.

There was no such attention paid to the body of Henry Gale, which lay at an odd angle over a tipped wooden chair, eyes open as if gazing at the prairie's wide sky.

"My husband was long ago forgiven," Mrs. Richter said.

None dared speak.

"Forgiven by me," she said. "And forgiven by the Lord. Just look around at my husband's good works. Look around! Ask anyone."

Mayor Watt-Smith expressed his sympathies. "He will be with the angels . . ."

But Dr. Wilford offered to the poor woman something else. Cruel calumny. "Forgiven for the child, you mean?"

Mrs. Richter fixed Dr. Wilford with furious eyes.

We ought not to have been surprised by the Wilford woman's indecency. Nonetheless, we were taken aback when she pressed Mrs. Richter even further. "Alvina Clough never forgave him, never relieved him of his responsibilities, his guilt." Dr. Wilford's voice was soft and companionable, but her intentions were of a different stripe.

"My husband did no harm to that Clough woman." Mrs. Richter snapped, pointing a bloody finger at Dr. Wilford. "He *never* did a thing except suffer. For years." Her voice shook and her eyes widened. Her grief transformed into rage. Poor thing. Then that rage turned to madness.

What Mrs. Richter said next to the Wilford woman was spoken in a state of shock and could not be taken as truth.

"The hag pressed him, but never quite far enough to cross a line. Until that letter—I found it slipped under the church door. He never even saw it. If he had, he'd just have placated her once again. *I* poisoned her. And two nights later *I* burned off her wretched face, getting *both* of those accursed ghosts out of his life. The hag and the bastard. For the good of us all! Imagine what this brilliant man could have done. Imagine how many people he could have helped."

"Please, Mrs. Richter," the mayor said, taking her by the wrist, "you're talking nonsense."

"You're in shock, dear," the doctor said.
Mrs. Richter yanked her hand out of the mayor's grasp and set it hard on her husband's blood-soaked chest. She looked again at Dr. Wilford and with a quick throwing motion spattered the woman with her husband's still-warm blood.

For a moment it seemed Dr. Wilford might collapse. Her expression shifted from surprise to fear. We couldn't tell if it was Mrs. Richter's delirious fabrications or the reverend's blood splashed across her gown that addled the ordinarily composed out-of-towner. Frankly, we didn't care. Tears coursed down her face, but we were not deceived. As it says in Proverbs: *"A continual dropping on a very rainy day and a contentious woman are alike."*

Then Mrs. Richter collapsed onto her husband's body.

By now, most of the women who remained in the hall with the overturned benches and chairs were also weeping. Those with husbands or grown sons were tenderly comforted.

Widows and maidens comforted one another. But the reality of our community's loss was only beginning to set in. To say nothing of the tragic personal catastrophe suffered by the much loved and admired Mrs. Richter, whose feverish words had been heard only by those gathered around the reverend in his last moments.

Would our town ever be the same?

Mayor Watt-Smith pointed to Henry Gale's body. "Somebody do something about that."

The quartet of men took it upon themselves to move the body out of sight.

Mrs. Richter didn't speak another word that night. The next day, when she sat up in bed and asked Dr. Ward to recount the events of the evening, she didn't recall one syllable of the delusional confession she'd made in the moments following her husband's death. None of us had the heart to tell her about her temporary derangement—the result of her grief. What did it matter now?

★　★　★

In the first fervid moments after the shootings, the letter that Dr. Wilford had read aloud to the gathering disappeared. Who can say what happened to it? Perhaps in the scuttling and scattering of panicked townsfolk, the papers got knocked to the ground, where any random treading might have destroyed or displaced them. Their whereabouts were not the focus of our attention at the time. Not with our reverend dying before us, his wife's mind cracking, and the acrid stench of gunpowder still in the air. What did the disappearance matter in the end? While the mayor and Dr. Ward seemed to recognize the handwriting as Alvina's, the thing could just as easily have been a counterfeit. We hadn't considered such a duplicitous possibility at the time, but as things played out regarding Dr. Evelyn Grace Wilford, we learned that almost nothing was beyond her malicious intentions.

As for the maliciousness of Henry Gale . . .

We'd never believed him capable of lethal violence against an innocent man. He never made a success of his farm, but neither did he lose it, as some of his contemporaries lost theirs. And while he was neither a model husband nor uncle, he never beat Emily or the girl. What then had propelled him to such evil? It is difficult not to blame Dr. Wilford's reckless disregard for our town, the truth, and God's good ways. Yes, Henry Gale carried within him a spiteful envy that had distanced him for years from the heartening moral assistance offered by our community. And after the twister, he'd taken to drink. But all this explains only his unpleasantness, not murder. It had to be Dr. Wilford's degrading implications about the years of charitable care Henry had offered his orphaned niece that pushed him to kill. What must those slanderous assertions about payments from Alvina Clough have sounded like to him? To this day, it remains a mystery why he did not put the bullet into Dr. Wilford's breast rather than the reverend's. We'll never know. Henry is dead and the Wilford woman is gone.

During the sleepless night that followed the melee, we attended to the stricken widow, to the transport of the bodies, and to the restoration of calm. Others of us moved from the church hall to the church itself and commenced singing hymns. The reverend would have been proud. We paid no attention to the Wilford woman, who drifted away from the scene at some point. Since the sheriff told us we hadn't sufficient cause to arrest her, we were glad she was gone. Some among us even claimed they would have committed violence upon her if she had remained. And more violence was not what we needed in those first hours. What we needed was healing, not justice. Not yet, at least. Still, news and rumor began spreading even before sunrise, the most illuminative of which came from Patterson, the hotel manager, who told us he had cleaned the Wilford woman's room the previous day and had discovered among her possessions a deck of Tarot cards. Patterson was a reliable man, so the news sent chills through us. The Wilford woman practiced divination? I needn't elaborate on the good book's teachings regarding such abominations. We were horrified, but not surprised. 1 Peter warns, *"Your adversary the devil, as a roaring lion, walketh about, seeking whom he may devour."* Alas, we recognized only too late whom she served. As a result of this oversight, we had shown her nothing but acceptance, hospitality, and even friendship. Today, we take comfort for our mistakes only in this: we failed not in our hearts, but in our heads, which is where the Devil may make mayhem even for good Christians.

The next morning the town was eerily still. Shocked. Exhausted. Grieving.

It was noon when we called at the hotel for the Wilford woman. By then she'd been gone many hours; or perhaps she'd never returned from the church hall to the room. Her clothing hung in the chiffonier, and her suitcase remained on a stool at the foot of the bed. It contained additional personal items and, yes, Tarot cards. Illustrated with decadent images, these vile tools of Satan are not illegal, but they are evidence of wickedness. Also damning were three long letters she had begun writing the night of her arrival in Sunbonnet and had continued scribbling right up to the hour she left her room for the fateful

Bible meeting. These letters were addressed to a former professor, famous in his field, and they described in a dark manner
her brief time in our town, twisting facts and implying evil
among *us*. We piled the pages together and delivered the stack
to the mayor, who said he would see to its proper filing. Some
cabinet in Hell, we thought.

But where was the woman herself?

No morning train had stopped at the station, as it was
Thursday. The men at the livery reported she had hired no
wagon. We were at a loss for how she made her way out of
town. It was only the next day, when someone thought to go
to the Gale farm to inquire after Emily's health and to inform
her of Henry's shameful act and subsequent death, that we
inferred the truth.

This is what we put together.

Dr. Wilford walked directly from the church hall to the
Gale farm in the moonlit hours immediately after the catastrophe. Three miles. Not so far, especially for one fueled by diabolical intent. There, she must have awakened poor,
broken-down Emily, who could not speak but could hear and
understand, to tell her what had happened. Or her version of it.
There's no guessing what untruths characterized her report to
the damaged woman. In any case, she convinced Emily to help
her hook the team to the Gale's wagon, and in the dead of
night, they drove onto the road and out from town, passing
between the silent, furrowed rows of neighbors' farms. We
hadn't any clue to their destination. What seems obvious now
didn't occur to us at the time.

We ought to have informed state authorities about what
happened in the church hall and the disappearance of the two
women. But our initial impulse, born of Christian concern for

the most shocked among us, was to limit communal damage by addressing the aftermath of the violence ourselves. Henry Gale was dead, and there was no need for a trial. We saw no advantage to making a state case of it. We knew better than to invite more newspapermen. The last thing poor Mrs. Richter needed in the early days of her widowhood was to be subjected to suspicion and scrutiny. We were frankly relieved to discover both the Wilford woman and Emily Gale were gone. We chose not to alert state authorities to their disappearance because no charges could have been brought against them anyway. Emily Gale may have been crippled by her seizure, but she remained in the eyes of the law an unencumbered woman, free to do as she pleased. Since there is no statute forbidding general turpitude or deceit, the Wilford woman couldn't be arrested for her actions in Sunbonnet. We didn't know what was to come in Topeka. It goes without saying that if we had, we'd have alerted the authorities immediately.

It was close to three weeks before we learned that Dr. Wilford and Emily Gale made a brief stop in Wichita the day after their departure from Sunbonnet. There, the deceitful woman sent a telegram to the same professor to whom she had addressed the never-delivered letters we found in her hotel room. Police investigators determined that the three-line wire had served to dupe the professor into calling upon his professional renown to persuade the Topeka Insane Asylum to grant Dr. Wilford permission to remove Dorothy Gale for a therapeutic ride in a hired carriage. This ride proved instead to be a kidnapping. Investigators learned in the days after Dorothy's disappearance that Dr. Wilford, Emily Gale, and the eleven-year-old girl had boarded a train in Topeka bound for Chicago. From there, the trail went cold. We shuddered at the horrific prospect of a crippled woman and her deranged niece being under the sway and command of one as treacherous as Dr. Wilford.

Hope for their discovery persists.

Investigators found no sign that the trio ever stopped at Dr. Wilford's residence, located in the moneyed neighborhood of Beacon Street in Boston. We weren't surprised that the Wilford woman had come from ease and luxury. Her willfulness and lack of moral backbone indicated as much. These financial resources suggested to authorities that the fugitives may have fled the country. To this day we pray for Emily, who is not to blame for the terrible moment when her husband was moved to violence by Dr. Wilford's deceitful public provocations. We pray too for Dorothy. Who knows what might become of her now?

As for us, we endure.

The funeral for our devoted minister and friend, Ralph Richter, was conducted by Reverend Thomas Hartley, the pastor of a small but devout congregation in Pratt. Our entire town attended the service. Owing to the turnout, it was held outdoors in the park across the street from the church. The weather was beautiful, and we couldn't help but be reminded of how often our Lord preached in grassy places like this. Yes, we felt the presence of Jesus. Some among us were inspired to recall stories of Ralph Richter's willingness to give of his time to congregants in need. Others spoke of his extraordinary learning and down-to-earth way of sharing it with us. Some made gentle humor of his disheveled office. And more than a few spoke movingly of Mrs. Richter, the loving and supportive partner. Our hearts were broken for her, and we offered our warmth and open arms. In the end, the afternoon uplifted, refreshed, and healed us. We realized we'd always carry within us his charitable and devout spirit. We are at peace knowing that as much as he loved our town, he is now in an even better place.

A few days after the service Henry Gale was buried in an unmarked but respectable plot paid for with proceeds from the sale of his farm. A handful of the town's most notable men attended the graveside service. It was also conducted by Reverend Hartley, who, within a month arranged for reassignment from his congregation in Pratt to join us in the church that Reverend Richter had built. He had been moved by what he saw of our town's generosity and Christian devotion in a time of tribulation. He is a great gift to us. His wife too has proved a wonder at restoring our spirit of joyful community. Mrs. Richter, always welcome among us, chose after the funeral to return to her family's home in Indianapolis. She bravely bears her widowhood even as she cares for her septuagenarian parents. The selflessness of her decision did not surprise us.

And so, Sunbonnet has once more become what it was always meant to be: a town where simple, God-fearing folk may live together in peace and prosperity. We are Kansans. We are Americans. We have survived a period of diabolical attack led by an eleven-year-old girl and a woman doctor from the east, both fine of feature but black of heart. They are gone. We remain. And with the Lord's help we will thrive.

CHAPTER 17

October 2, 1896

Dear Cousin Frank,

We are mid-Atlantic on a cloudless day aboard the SS *New York*, due into Southampton tomorrow evening. Once there I will post this letter, and by the time it makes its way to your warm and welcoming home, Dorothy, Emily, and I will have left England and traveled on to the continent. As I suspect you will be contacted by authorities, I will not put you in legal jeopardy by further detailing our movements or the city where I have arranged for us to settle. Suffice to say that locales of great interest, particularly to one like myself with a vocation for psychology, lie ahead. You'll also be relieved to know that I transferred my assets into a Swiss account before leaving the States. Strange how easy it is to abandon a whole life. Strange too that I will miss so little of it. Of course, I will miss you, Frank, my favorite cousin (bolder of spirit than any of us). And I will miss Maude and your beautiful children. And yes, Professor James, I'll miss him too. Perhaps one day, when the authorities lose interest in me, I'll be able to write him and apologize for having misused his good name for my own ends, however justified. I hope he will understand that if I had admitted to him my actual intentions, I'd have implicated him in the crime. That I lied is his best defense. I still cannot contact him without delivering to his door a legal and moral quandary. But that is a matter for another time. In his book he wrote, "The deepest principle in human nature is the craving to be appreciated." If you should happen to see him on one of your visits east, please let him know how very much he is appreciated. And also that I am well prepared now to be on my own.

There is much good to report. Dorothy is recovering well from her time in the asylum and has regained much of the strength and some of the weight she lost there. Her psyche seems to have held up. She is as bright and generous of spirit as I believed. Though she maintains her detailed delusion about the days she went missing in Kansas, she shows no other signs of mental aberration. Some children have imaginary friends. It is something they outgrow. What is the harm? And if she never outgrows the delusion . . . well, what a fine adventure she will have to remember! I look across the stateroom now and watch her with her aunt. It is inspiring to see the warmth and care that Dorothy offers Emily, who is making good progress in her recovery. Dorothy and I work with her every day on exercises to help her regain her speech and use of her right arm. We three are good traveling companions. We are often mistaken by other passengers for a family—grandmother, mother, and young daughter. Oh yes, and the family dog, Toto. We never correct them. Nor will we do so in the future, in our new lives. It provides good cover. And it doesn't feel so far from true.

I am sorry for the hurried letter I sent to you from Topeka, when every second seemed to count and any false move felt potentially disastrous. I had spent many hours in Sunbonnet documenting in long letters to Professor James my interviews with the principals, my view of the town, and my increasingly specific suspicions. I was forced to abandon those documents, along with all of my traveling clothes and kit, when I chose not to return to the hotel, but to walk straight to the Gale farm. I managed only the hurried, incomplete summary I sent to you. I'm afraid I haven't the will now to flesh it out further. More specifically, I haven't the will to revisit events. That final evening still weighs heavily upon my mind. The church hall was a war zone. In real life, shootings are not as they are in dime novels. Being the natural storyteller you are, I'm sure I've left you with many questions. The best I can do is hope that one day we can sit together so I can answer them.

Still, you are sufficiently informed to see how the "disappearance" of Alvina's letter, the death of both the reverend and Mr. Gale, and the self-serving conspiracy of silence among townsfolk leaves no place for further action in Sunbonnet. There is no proving any legal charge, no substantiating a newspaper story. The widowed Mrs. Richter is untouchable. Is my failure to have identified her as a suspect, when she had access to the same information as her husband, part of the habitual devaluation of women's capacities? If so, it is, sadly, not the greatest of my offenses. Reverend Richter, a hypocrite but no murderer, is dead. As is Henry Gale. And I bear blame for those deaths. Oh, Frank, am I a good witch or a bad witch?

But I won't allow myself to dwell on that sort of question.

Instead, I must remind myself of what motivated me in the first place: saving Dorothy from the terrible fate that threatened her in the asylum. True, you may say I could have used my position and academic connections to "kidnap" her on the

very first day I met her. The truth is I never would have
dreamed of doing such a thing. Not until I proved *to myself* that
she was innocent. This I accomplished. I also freed Emily from
a blighted existence. The future is bright for the two. It is there
that I will place my energies.

One other detail still possesses me.

I doubt that I mentioned in my hurried letter to you that
when Alvina Clough returned from her year "abroad," she dis-
tributed souvenirs of Europe to important townsfolk, a ploy to
conceal the true purpose of her absence. This much makes
sense. But Sheriff Hutchins mentioned to me that he spied one
of these souvenirs in the wreckage of Dorothy's room and
wondered at that time why Alvina would have bothered to
make a gift to a family of such little importance. The answer is
obvious now. Alvina was mother to the child. It was a covert
gift to her daughter. But would a monster be moved to do such
a thing? This poses another question. Might Alvina have
arranged and paid for Dorothy's deceitful rearing to be *in Sunbonnet* not out of a perverse cruelty or need for control (as the
reverend and his wife doubtless believed), but because she
wanted to keep her daughter near her, even if she could never
acknowledge her? And what of the behest? And what of the
urgent threat that Alvina issued in her letter to the reverend to
find the girl's body before it was defiled by animals? Taking
into account all I have learned of Sunbonnet, perhaps these
things were all any mother could be expected to do for her
child under scandalous circumstances. And if this is so . . . then
who really was Alvina Clough? The model of wretchedness
and pure selfishness collapses, and we are left with a woman we
do not know. One we can never know. A woman in full. So,
when there comes an appropriate time to describe Alvina to

Dorothy, I will say, "She loved you," because it may well have been true.

    My warmest to Maud and the children,
    Yours,
    Evie

P.S. On deck yesterday, we three made the acquaintance of the great author Samuel Clemens, his lovely wife, Olivia, and one of their grown daughters. Dorothy related details of her Oz adventure to Mr. Clemens, and he was so impressed that he said if he hadn't already gotten his fill of writing children's books, he'd steal her story and publish it himself. I suspect he was only being genial. But it got me thinking. You are a man of great imagination, Frank, wholly unappreciated in the newspaper trade. And seeing as the chickens and playwriting didn't work out, perhaps Mr. Clemens's idea isn't so bad. You already know details of the Oz story from covering Dorothy's hearing in Sunbonnet. I asked Dorothy if she'd mind if you made a book out of it, and she was delighted by the idea. Her only request is that you make her return to Kansas at the end of the story, omitting all that occurred afterward. I believe you could write something lovely, Frank. You deserve a good break too. Just an idea . . .

AFTER *AFTER OZ*

Experience teaches us again and again that life is not fair.
I was reminded of this fact when, on November 24, 2021, I received a horrible if not unexpected piece of news: Gordon McAlpine, author of—among other books—the Edgar Award–nominated *Woman With a Blue Pencil*, had lost his fight with cancer.

Gordon began chemotherapy and immunotherapy in November 2020. A little over a year later, in concert with his wife, Julie, and his sons, Harlan, Shane and Jonathan, Gordon made the decision to go into hospice care.

Gordon knew the beauty of this world, of being alive in it, and he approached cancer as he approached so many things—as an opportunity to appreciate and celebrate the here and now. No doubt anger and fear and sorrow were also part of his response but, knowing Gordon, I'd bet they didn't predominate. They'd have just been there, part of the experience.

In 2013, I purchased a copy of Gordon's *Hammett Unwritten* on a visit to the Mysterious Bookshop. I'd read a review in *Mystery Scene* and decided to take a chance. I had no idea that Gordon would become a cherished friend and that I'd adapt one of his books (*Holmes Entangled*) for the stage. I knew right away, however, that he was a fine and imaginative writer—I knew that from the start. We first met when he was in New York City for an event at the Center for Fiction. We started corresponding, and a friendship was born.

Like so many others who knew Gordon, I wanted more time with this wonderful man; more long, leisurely lunches on his trips to Manhattan; more conversations; more books. I hope we've all found solace in the memory of his understated bravery, his generous and open heart, his capacity for hope, and his wisdom: he loved this world so dearly that his graciousness and sense of dignity told him when it was time to leave it.

So harsh was his loss that one is apt to overlook the fact that he left us with a handful of gems, those magical works of his imagination. *After Oz* is now his last novel, not merely his latest. *Oz* combines his love of literary legerdemain with his sympathy for the outsider and a mystery with a solution straight out of the Golden Age of Queen and Carr and Christie. As his readers know, Gordon loved to mix genres.

In March 2019, Gordon wrote to me: "I've just today typed 'THE END' to *Dorothy Gale, Kansas*"—the book's original title. "It's exceeded my expectations in many ways. For example, despite its historical setting it's very much of our times. No one's read it yet, so I may be wrong . . ." Gordon was right. His story about hatred and bigotry and the struggle between the liberal imagination and the closed mind is indeed "very much of our times." As an allegory for this fractious and troubled world, his book was (and remains) right on target.

When Gordon was next in NYC, we had lunch at Bar Six. He told me something I'd never known about the Judy Garland film. The moment the black-and-white Dorothy, seen from behind, opens the door to reveal the saturated *color* of the land of Oz is one of the unforgettable moments in the MGM adaptation. Gordon revealed just how that trick had been accomplished. The back of Judy Garland's double and the inside of the farmhouse were painted in sepia tones but filmed in color; when the black-and-white Dorothy steps out of the frame, Judy steps in, opens the door, and there we are in the extravagantly hued merry old land of Oz. It's a simple but sophisticated trick. No wonder Gordon took such delight in it. His work partakes of a similar kind of elegant sleight of hand.

After Oz is also the most emotionally resonant of his novels. Everyone knows *The Wizard of Oz*. It's imprinted on generations of readers and/or viewers of the 1939 film, a direct conduit to the marvelous and the frightening—to childhood. Gordon's approach respects the deep feelings engendered by Baum's work and provides us with a startlingly fresh look at Dorothy Gale and her world. It's a brilliant idea, and he carried it out with skill and love.

Life is unfair, without a doubt. But it is also beautiful, and sometimes it offers us beautiful surprises. *After Oz* is one of them.

Joseph Goodrich
Jackson Heights, NY

December 2023

Joseph Goodrich is an Edgar Award–winning playwright and the author of the novel *The Paris Manuscript*. His plays have been produced around the country, as well as in Canada, Australia, and China. His fiction and nonfiction have appeared in *Ellery Queen's Mystery Magazine, Alfred Hitchcock's Mystery Magazine, Noir Riot*, and two Mystery Writers of America anthologies. An alumnus of New Dramatists and a Calderwood Fellow at MacDowell, he is a graduate of Hamline University.

ACKNOWLEDGMENTS

As a child Gordon found solace in the bountiful world of imagination. He loved books, movies, and music; he lived most fully inside them, and they remained indelibly inside him. *The Wizard of Oz* was a magical experience for many of us as children. But Gordon, as with so many things he discovered early in his life, examined the film and novel as an adult, to understand his fascination.

Twenty years ago we were in Big Sur when the idea of exploring Dorothy's life after Oz in the form of a novel began to percolate. How do you go back to your "ordinary" life after experiencing Oz? In retrospect, I think Gordon was examining the life of an artist who lives inside his imagination and the callings of "ordinary" life. The book roamed around his mind as other ideas were realized. Over time, the influence of the more current political climate took hold, and the novel was developed in that context.

I know Gordon would want to acknowledge first and foremost L. Frank Baum, Victor Fleming, and Judy Garland for their timeless work. On Gordon's behalf I want to thank Joe Goodrich for his masterful editing, moving Afterword, and great friendship. I want to especially thank Lukas Ortiz for his unwavering support of Gordon's novels and his grace as an agent and friend. It is Lukas who brought this book to life.

As always, Gordon would acknowledge his three boys, now men: Jonathan, Shane, and Harlan—it was through his sons that he found the beauty and joy in everyday life; and our dogs, Finnegan and Diego, who were by his side for the writing of this book and beyond.

Ultimately, I believe he would acknowledge the world of imagination—its beauty and poignancy, its allure and dangers.